SWORD ART ONLINE
ALICIZATION RISING
012

REKI KAWAHARA
ABEC
bee-pee

SWORD ART ONLINE

"It has been two years since I last bathed in the fire of my Conflagration Bow. I can see that you have the skill to match Eldrie Thirty-One indeed, sinners."

Deusolbert Synthesis Seven § An Integrity Knight and wielder of the Conflagration Bow.

"I'll find some way to stop that first shot, and then you hack away at him, Eugeo."

Kirito § A boy who found himself within a mysterious fantasy realm. He seeks the system console that will allow him to escape.

"All right."

Eugeo § The first resident of this world whom Kirito met. A fellow elite disciple of Kirito's at the North Centoria Imperial Swordcraft Academy.

"And now I bid you farewell, young, foolish heretic. Hidden light of the Heaven-Piercing Blade, cast off your shackles!! Release Recollection!!"

Fanatio Synthesis Two § Vice commander of the Integrity Knights and wielder of the Heaven-Piercing Blade.

"Very well. I shall ascertain the nature of your wickedness from the way you fight."

Alice Synthesis Thirty § An Integrity Knight and wielder of the Osmanthus Blade.

"Kirito, student of the sword, seeks a proper duel of blade against blade with the Integrity Knight Alice!"

CENTRAL CATHEDRAL

Within the Underworld, Centoria is the capital city, located directly in the center of the human realm. At the heart of the city, and thus all of humanity, is the massive white Central Cathedral tower. Its pinnacle is so high that it can barely be seen, and looming walls hide the square grounds of the church from sight. The Axiom Church is the organization presiding over the entire human race. Its military officials, known as Integrity Knights, are tasked with maintaining order and serve as inspiration to the training swordfighters, who look up to them.

The cathedral is one hundred floors in height, the top floor housing the chamber of the Axiom Church's pontifex. The middle floors are where the Church's administrative agents, such as monks and priests, manage the affairs of humanity. There is also an armory on the third floor and the Great Hall of Ghostly Light on the fiftieth floor.

Illustration: Tatsuya Kurusu

SWORD ART ONLINE

ALICIZATION RISING

VOLUME 12

Reki Kawahara

abec

bee-pee

YEN ON

NEW YORK

SWORD ART ONLINE, Volume 12: ALICIZATION RISING
REKI KAWAHARA

Translation by Stephen Paul
Cover art by abec

SWORD ART ONLINE
©REKI KAWAHARA 2013
Edited by ASCII MEDIA WORKS
First published in Japan in 2013 by KADOKAWA CORPORATION, Tokyo.
English translation rights arranged with KADOKAWA CORPORATION, Tokyo,
through Tuttle-Mori Agency, Inc., Tokyo.

English translation © 2017 by Yen Press, LLC

Yen On
1290 Avenue of the Americas
New York, NY 10104

Visit us at yenpress.com
facebook.com/yenpress
twitter.com/yenpress
yenpress.tumblr.com
instagram.com/yenpress

First Yen On Edition: December 2017

Yen On is an imprint of Yen Press, LLC.
The Yen On name and logo are trademarks of Yen Press, LLC.

Library of Congress Cataloging-in-Publication Data
Names: Kawahara, Reki, author. | Abec, 1985– illustrator. | Paul, Stephen,
    translator.
Title: Sword art online / Reki Kawahara, abec ; translation, Stephen Paul.
Description: First Yen On edition. | New York, NY : Yen On, 2014–
Identifiers: LCCN 2014001175 | ISBN 9780316371247 (v. 1 : pbk.) | ISBN 9780316376815
    (v. 2 : pbk.) | ISBN 9780316296427 (v. 3 : pbk.) | ISBN 9780316296434 (v. 4 : pbk.)
    | ISBN 9780316296441 (v. 5 : pbk.) | ISBN 9780316296458 (v. 6 : pbk.) | ISBN
    9780316390408 (v. 7 : pbk.) | ISBN 9780316390415 (v. 8 : pbk.) | ISBN 9780316390422
    (v. 9 : pbk.) | ISBN 9780316390439 (v. 10 : pbk.) | ISBN 9780316390446 (v. 11 : pbk.) |
    ISBN 9780316390453 (v. 12 : pbk.)
Subjects: | CYAC: Science fiction. | BISAC: FICTION / Science Fiction / Adventure.
Classification: pz7.K1755Ain 2014 | DDC [Fic]—dc23
LC record available at https://lccn.loc.gov/2014001175

ISBNs: 978-0-316-39045-3 (paperback)
        978-0-316-56104-4 (ebook)

10 9 8 7 6 5 4 3 2 1

LSC-C

Printed in the United States of America

"THIS MIGHT BE A GAME, BUT IT'S NOT SOMETHING YOU PLAY."

—Akihiko Kayaba, *Sword Art Online* programmer

SWORD ART ONLINE
ALICIZATION RISING

Reki Kawahara

abec

bee-pee

CHAPTER SEVEN

TWO ADMINISTRATORS, MAY 380 HE

1

It was on November 7th, 2024 that I—Kazuto Kirigaya—escaped from the VRMMORPG named *Sword Art Online*.

In mid-December, I finished my physical rehabilitation and returned home to the city of Kawagoe in Saitama Prefecture. Two months before that had been my sixteenth birthday, but while all my old classmates were studying to get into high school, I'd been busy delving into the labyrinth tower of the fiftieth floor of Aincrad, completely cut off from all formal education.

Fortunately (if you can call it that), my middle school sympathetically offered me a graduation diploma, despite the fact that I'd finished only half my credits. As long as I took some cram school courses, I should have been ready to tackle high school a year late—until the government offered me an unexpected source of salvation.

Of the roughly six thousand people who returned from *SAO* alive, over five hundred were in middle or high school. In April 2025, the government opened a special school just for them in west Tokyo, free of entrance requirements or tuition, with the promise of college entrance–exam eligibility once we graduated.

They reused a condemned municipal high school campus that had been waiting for demolition since the previous year. Many of the teachers commissioned to work there had already been retired. It was officially classified as a national specialty school.

The comprehensiveness of this safety net paradoxically filled me with concern, but after consulting with my family and, of course, Asuna, I decided to enroll. Never once did I regret that decision. Designing and creating various devices with my new friends in the mechatronics course was great fun, and I got to see Asuna, Lisbeth, and Silica every day. Even with the mandatory weekly counseling session, it was a fulfilling school life.

But once again, I was unable to finish my education.

One year and two months after enrolling, in June of 2026, I found that my mind had been whisked into the alternate realm known as the Underworld through means unknown. After waking up in the forest near a village named Rulid at the far northern stretches of the human territory, I tried in vain to contact the employees of Rath, the company that developed and operated the Underworld, and received no answer.

That left me no choice but to attempt to reach a system console that might allow me to contact the outside world—a device that could only be in Central Cathedral, a tower that belonged to the Axiom Church and loomed over everything in the land of Centoria, the very heart of the human realm. Thus, I set out on a long journey from Rulid with my partner, Eugeo, the very first person I'd met in this world.

After an entire year, by the calendar of the Underworld, we reached Centoria but did not make it straight into the cathedral. The Church kept its gates locked shut, letting in only the champion of the annual Four-Empire Unification Tournament.

And so Eugeo and I, chasing the same goal for different reasons, started at the Imperial Swordcraft Academy in the hopes of winning the right to compete in that very tournament. The classes were almost all based on swordfighting and magic (or *sacred arts*, as they called them), so it was a curriculum I'd never experienced in the real world. That, combined with the novelty of living in a dorm, made my stay at the academy an interesting one...even enjoyable, in a way.

But a year and a month after starting school, in May of the year 380 in the Human Empire calendar, disaster struck, and my schooling came to an abrupt end. Two male students of elite noble lineage set up a clever trap to abuse and assault Ronie and Tiese, our personal pages.

When he discovered the ugly scene, Eugeo managed to break loose from the shackles that compelled all Underworldians to follow the law, and he drew his sword. He severed noble Humbert's left arm, and when I arrived, I fought with Raios and cut off both his hands.

Despite these wounds, both should have survived if they stopped the bleeding and underwent emergency sacred arts healing, but something very strange happened: Forced to choose between following the Taboo Index that dictated law in this world and preserving his own life, Raios let out an inhuman wail and perished...or, more accurately, froze still.

Eugeo and I were banished from the school and led to the dungeon beneath Central Cathedral by an Integrity Knight dispatched by the Church. Undeterred by my third consecutive dropping out of school, I broke us free, and we wandered the rose garden within the cathedral grounds in search of a way into the tower itself. We wound up in battle against a new Integrity Knight and, in our most desperate moment, found salvation from an unlikely source: a strange little girl named Cardinal.

Living in a mammoth library that was sealed from the inside, Cardinal sent Eugeo to a hot bath to recover from getting dumped into a fountain during battle, and then took me aside to reveal the stunning truth.

The Underworld itself was a simulation of an entire civilization that had been running for over 450 internal years.

And the pontifex, the supreme commander of the almighty Axiom Church, was once a beautiful girl named Quinella, a resident of this place just like any other.

She mastered the sacred arts—in other words, the program's system commands—and, in her never-ending thirst for power, finally unearthed the full command list. It launched her from a simple active agent—a unit within the simulation—into a full-blown system administrator.

With her absolute control over the Underworld, Quinella was up on the top floor of Central Cathedral even now, looking down on the world. But could she see me, the interloper who had wandered into her sacred garden...?

I felt a sudden chill rack my body. On the other side of the round table, Cardinal gave me a pained look. She took a sip of tea from her cup and adjusted her little spectacles. "It's too early to tremble in fear."

Somehow, I managed to dispel the cold. "Right...right. Please continue." I lifted my own cup and slurped the tea, which tasted a lot like real-world coffee.

The small girl leaned back in her chair and resumed her explanation in her easygoing way. "Two hundred and seventy years ago, after Quinella succeeded at calling up the entire command list, the first thing she did was raise her own Authority level to the maximum, which allowed her to affect the world-controlling Cardinal System itself. Next, she conferred all rights and privileges afforded only to Cardinal to herself: manipulating terrain and buildings; generating items; altering the durability of all mobile units, including human beings...in other words, meddling with their life itself..."

"Manipulating...life. In other words, changing the limit of one's life span..." I gasped. The little sage nodded.

"She had broken through. The first thing Quinella did as administrator, at the age of eighty and on death's door, was to completely restore her own life value. Then she stopped its natural decay process and returned her physical appearance to the radiant beauty of her late teens. You are still young, and male to boot—I daresay you cannot fathom the nature of her triumphant joy..."

"Well...I understand that it's one of the wildest dreams of any woman, I suppose," I said, straight-faced. Cardinal snorted.

"I don't even have human emotions, and I'm glad that my features are fixed in this state. Though if I'm being honest, I'd like to advance by five or six years...At any rate, Quinella's bliss at having all her ravenous desires fulfilled was nearly unfathomable. She was able to freely control the vast reach of the Human Empire and had attained eternal youth and beauty. Her jubilation was...sheer madness. Enough to loosen, just by a bit, her grasp on sanity..."

Behind the lenses, Cardinal's big eyes narrowed. They seemed to mock the foolishness of humanity—or perhaps pity it.

"She ought to have been happy with that. But the hole that had opened in Quinella's heart was bottomless. She didn't know how to be satisfied...and so she decided she could not condone the existence of the one with privilege equal to hers."

"Meaning...the Cardinal System itself?"

"None other. Indeed, she attempted to eliminate a program without a conscious will of its own. But...no matter how advanced her sacred arts were, Quinella was nothing more than an Underworldian, far from a resident of a scientific culture. She could not fathom in a single night the workings of admin-level command structures. Quinella attempted in vain to decipher the reference materials saved for Rath engineers...and she made a mistake. One simple but enormous mistake. She decided to absorb the Cardinal System itself and chanted a mammoth string of sacred arts. And as a result..."

She breathed out a sigh, the words tumbling free with her breath.

"...Quinella burned the prime directive of the Cardinal System into her own fluctlight, as her own behavioral principle, in a way that can't be overwritten. She meant to steal its authority level alone, but instead, she fused her very soul with Cardinal!"

"...Uh...wh-what...?" I mumbled, unable to grasp this concept in the moment. "What exactly is Cardinal's...prime directive...?"

"The upholding of order. It is the very reason for the Cardinal System's existence. I'm sure you understand, having been in the world controlled by that system. Cardinal is constantly observing the actions of all players like yourself. When it detects a phenomenon that disrupts the balance of the world, it acts mercilessly to correct it."

"Yeah...that's true. I've spent plenty of time trying to get the better of Cardinal, but every time I thought I found a hole, it was always plugged instantly..."

I recalled all the times back in *SAO* when I thought I'd hit upon a new farming technique, only for it to fail within moments. Cardinal, the girl in front of me, grinned proudly. This expression was the only moment when she truly went from being a wizened sage to the mischievous girl that her appearance suggested.

"But of course. You little whelps can't possibly get the better of me, no matter how many of you there are...But Quinella's upholding of order was far more extreme. With these orders now written into her fluctlight, she passed out, and did not wake for an entire day. By then, she was no longer human in any sense of the word. Never aging, drinking, eating...her only desire was to preserve for eternity the world she ruled over..."

"Preserve...for eternity...," I mumbled, contemplating the idea.

Every manager of a VRMMO wishes for the game world to continue into perpetuity, not just the Cardinal System AI. It is why they fine-tune game economies, items, and monster rates—to maintain order. But there is one thing that a godlike administrator cannot entirely control: the players.

Could the same thing be said of the Underworld...?

Cardinal sensed my unspoken thought and bobbed her head. "Once, the Cardinal System of this world controlled just the flora and fauna, terrain, and climate. In other words, it managed only the container and allowed the artificial fluctlights within it to go about their lives unaffected...But Quinella was different.

She wanted to fix even the lives of her subjects into a permanent state."

"Fix? You mean like...making it so that everyone does the same thing every day, and nothing new ever happens...?"

"Well...I suppose you could put it that way. Continuing on... Once Quinella had fused with the Cardinal System, she gave herself a new identity. Now she was the pontifex, the highest officer of the Axiom Church...and her name would now be Administrator."

I jumped at the mention of that name. "Oh! Yeah, he said that name, too. The Integrity Knight Eldrie Synthesis...um..."

"Thirty-One."

"Right. He said something about how Administrator, the pontifex, had summoned him from the celestial world to the land... So he was talking about Quinella...It's, um, quite a name to give yourself."

To me, the English term *administrator* was more familiar in terms of computer control status—admin accounts, say—than its original meaning. But I couldn't be sure which definition Quinella had chosen it for.

Cardinal smirked briefly and nodded. "I suppose it is fitting that she would name herself after the gods of our world...But at any rate, she was now the administrator in both title and function, and her first edict was to elevate the four major noble lines of the time into emperors, and split the four directions into four empires. You have seen the walls that break Centoria into quadrants, I trust?"

I confirmed with a bob of my head. The Swordcraft Academy was in District Five of North Centoria, the capital of the Norlangarth Empire. From the dorm, I could see the chalk-white walls that rose higher than any building in the city. I was stunned when I first learned that those Everlasting Walls were all that separated us from the capitals of other empires.

"Those walls were not constructed by granite blocks, mined

and assembled over decades. The Administrator used her godly powers to summon them in an instant."

"...An...an *instant*?! Those walls?! That's got to be beyond the scope of sacred arts...Didn't that stun all the people of Centoria...?"

"Of course. That was the point. She used the power of the Cardinal System to impress fear into the hearts of the citizens. Through this mental barrier, and the literal barrier of the Everlasting Walls, she could limit the flow and mingling of the people. That way, the Axiom Church had control over the passage of information, and thus a better grip upon the people's minds. She wanted the people to be ignorant, pliable, faithful servants of the Church in perpetuity...And those preposterous walls weren't the only physical barriers she erected. In order to limit the frontier expansion happening in all directions, Administrator placed many massive terrain obstacles in their way—unbreakable rocks, bottomless swamps, uncrossable rapids, unfellable trees..."

"W-wait. Trees...you can't cut down?"

"Correct. A cedar of nearly unfathomable size, with practically unlimited priority and durability."

I thought of the tear-inducing hardness of the demonic Gigas Cedar and rubbed my palms together under the table.

So the Gigas Cedar wasn't a natural growth south of Rulid but an artificial roadblock placed by the Administrator, intended to prevent the residents from expanding their territory and activity by refusing to budge and sucking up local resources.

And there were other features like that out in the world. Things that people had wasted centuries of hard work in a futile attempt to eliminate...

When I looked up, the little girl was once again gazing at me with all-knowing eyes. Her tiny lips opened to continue the lesson.

"...And thus, under the control of the all-powerful Administrator, a very long time of peace and idleness came to pass. Twenty years, thirty...The people lost their spirit of ambition, the nobles fell into slovenly greed, and the heroic swordsmen of old sank to the level of a stage show. You have seen these things for yourself. For forty years, then fifty, Administrator gazed down at the lukewarm state of the human world and felt deep, deep satisfaction..."

It must have been like gazing upon the complete, pristine ecosystem of an aquarium. I recalled the fascinating entertainment I got from my ant farm kit as a boy and felt uncomfortable.

Cardinal reminisced as well, then glanced back at me and said firmly, "But there cannot be eternal stasis in any system. There are always events, incidents...Seventy years after Quinella became Administrator, she realized something had changed within her. Her conscious mind blanked out for short periods; even when she was awake, memories from the past few days became unavailable to her, and those perfectly memorized system commands wouldn't always spring to her tongue. These were grave phenomena. Administrator used her control commands to examine her own fluctlight in detail...and the results stunned her. She had reached the limit of her memory-holding capacity."

"L-limit?!" I yelped. This was a shock. I'd never heard that there was an upper limit to the amount of data—the amount of memory—a soul could hold.

"Is it so unbelievable? There is a physical limit to the size of the lightcube that holds a fluctlight, just as there is to a biological brain. Therefore, the number of quantum bits storing information is also limited," Cardinal explained matter-of-factly.

I held up my hand and pleaded, "W-wait, wait. Uh...you keep mentioning these 'lightcubes.' Am I supposed to believe the Underworldians' fluctlights are stored on those?"

"What, you didn't know that? A lightcube is an actual cube, two inches to a side. Each one is the exact size to contain a fluctlight, and the storage requires no system resources. They are gathered in what is called the Lightcube Cluster, measuring about ten feet to a side."

"S-so, uh...if they're two inches, then ten feet means...," I mumbled, trying to calculate the total number. Cardinal provided it for me.

"Theoretically, the total would be two hundred and sixteen thousand cubes. But because the Main Visualizer is contained at the center of the cluster, the actual number is fewer."

"Two hundred and sixteen thousand...So that's basically the upper limit of the Underworld's population..."

"Yes. And there's still plenty of room to go, so if you feel like finding a girl and adding to the number, there will be empty lightcubes to spare."

"Ahh...H-hey, who said anything about that?!" I protested. The young sage gave me a piercing look, then returned to the topic at hand.

"...However, as I mentioned, each lightcube will eventually reach its full capacity, given enough time. Administrator had already lived an impossible one and a half centuries since her birth as Quinella. The dam that contained all those years of memories finally began to leak, causing errors in her ability to save, store, and replay memories."

It was a chilling concept that struck home. I'd already built up two years of memory in this accelerated world. It would mean that even if I only spent months, or days, in here, my soul itself was still logging that information toward its eventual end.

"Have no fear. Your fluctlight still has plenty of blank space available," Cardinal pointed out with a smirk, reading my thoughts yet again.

"H-hey...that makes it sound like my head is totally empty..."

"If I am an encyclopedia, you are a picture book," she said smugly, taking a sip of tea and clearing her throat. "Continuing on. Faced with this unexpected issue of memory limits, the Administrator panicked. Unlike the easily controlled numerical value of life, this was a finite resource that could not be avoided. But she was not the kind of woman to accept this fate without a fight. Just as when she stole the throne of God, she came up with yet another diabolical solution..."

She grimaced, set her cup down, and folded her little cattleya-flower hands atop the table.

"...At the time...which was two hundred years ago, there was a girl studying sacred arts as a sister-in-training in the lower levels of Central Cathedral, a girl just ten years old. Her name...I have forgotten. She was born to a furniture maker in Centoria and, through the whims of random value settings, wound up with a slightly higher system access authority than others. Thus, she wound up selected for the Calling of a holy woman. A skinny, scrawny girl with brown eyes and brown curls..."

I blinked and reexamined Cardinal's appearance. She seemed to be describing herself.

"Administrator brought that girl to her chamber on the top floor of the cathedral and gave her the beatific smile of a holy mother. Then she said, 'You're going to be my child now. A child of God who will lead the world.' In a sense, she was right—in the sense that I would inherit the information of her soul. But it had nothing to do with the love of mother and child...Administrator attempted to overwrite that girl's fluctlight with her own fluct-light's thoughts and crucial memories."

"Wha...?"

Yet again, a chill crawled up my spine. *Overwriting the soul.* Even the phrase was horrifying. I rubbed my sweaty palms together and struggled to work my jaw into producing speech.

"B-but...if she's able to perform such complex fluctlight manipulations, why didn't she just erase the memories she didn't need?"

"Would you take your most important files and crack them open for editing?" she shot back. I faltered and had to shake my head.

"N-no...I'd make a backup first."

"Exactly. When the Administrator imprinted the Cardinal System's directives into her mind, she lost consciousness for a day and night. That is how dangerous manipulating one's own fluctlight is. What if one attempts to organize one's memories and causes damage to crucial data? Instead, she took over the soul of a young girl with plenty of extra memory capacity, and once she was satisfied that the replication worked, she planned to discard her original, worn-out soul. She was very thorough and very careful...but that is when the Administrator...when Quinella made her second great mistake."

"Mistake...?"

"Yes. Because when she took over the girl and scrapped her old self, there would be a single instant when there existed *two gods with equal power* at the same time. Administrator meticulously plotted and arranged a devilish ceremony...a fusing of soul and memory in what she called a Synthesis Ritual...and succeeded in seizing another fluctlight. I waited...how I waited for that moment...for seventy long years!!" she shouted, her features strained with slight agitation. I just stared at her, dumbfounded.

"Um...hang on. Then...who are you? Who's the Cardinal I'm talking to now?"

"Don't you understand yet?" she asked, pushing her glasses up. "You are familiar with my original version, Kirito? Tell me the features of the Cardinal System."

"Uh...well..."

I thought hard, summoning my memories of Aincrad. It was an autonomous management program that Akihiko Kayaba developed to run his game of death, *SAO*. Meaning...

"...It's meant to run automatically for long periods of time without human correction or maintenance...?"

"Indeed. And to achieve that..."

"To achieve that, it has two core programs—a main process that performs the balancing functions and a subprocess that performs error-checking on the main..."

I paused, my mouth hanging open, and stared at the little girl with the curly hair.

The Cardinal System's powerful error-correcting process should have been old news to me. Yui, the AI that Asuna and I took in as a daughter during our time in *SAO*, was a subordinate program of Cardinal, and I'd had to fight desperately to protect her when the system recognized her as foreign and mercilessly attempted to delete her.

In actual terms, I only accessed the *SAO* program space through the system console, searched for the files that made up Yui, compressed them, and turned them into an in-game object, but it was practically a miracle that I managed to do that much in the mere seconds that I had before Cardinal detected my access and shut me out. The massive presence that I was fighting on the other side of that holo-keyboard was Cardinal's error-correction process…meaning it was the sweet-looking girl sitting across from me now?

While I grappled with that complex rush of emotions, Cardinal sighed, as if dealing with a particularly dense child, and said, "You've finally put it together. It was not one single fundamental directive that Quinella wrote into her soul. The main process told her to *maintain the world*. And the subprocess ordered her…to *correct the mistakes of the main process*."

"Correct…the mistakes?"

"When I was an unconscious program, all I did was endlessly examine the data the main process spit out. But once I gained a personality as Quinella's 'shadow mind,' so to speak, I didn't just check for redundant code anymore; I had to judge my own actions. You might call it…multiple personalities."

"Then again, in the real world there are those who say that multiple personalities are a thing that only exists in fiction."

"Is that so? But it is very real to me. Only when Quinella's consciousness faltered the slightest bit could my cogitation process surface. And so I thought…this woman named Administrator has committed massive mistakes."

"A…mistake…?" I repeated. If maintaining the world was the basis of Cardinal's main process, it seemed that no matter how extreme Quinella's choices were, she was perfectly aligned with that directive.

But Cardinal stared right back into my eyes and intoned, "Then

I ask you. Did the Cardinal System in the world you knew ever once do direct harm to a player?"

"Er...no, it didn't. It was the player's ultimate enemy, yes...but it didn't unfairly attack any players directly. Sorry, point taken," I said. She snorted.

"But that is what she did. She meted out a punishment crueler than death to those who doubted her Taboo Index or expressed rebellion toward her order...but I will tell you about that in detail later. On those few occasions I awoke from my sleep as the Cardinal System's subprocess, I determined that Administrator's existence was one enormous error and attempted to destroy it. Three times I attempted to jump from the top floor of the tower, twice I tried to stab myself in the heart with a knife, and twice I used sacred arts to burn myself. If a single action could reduce her life to zero, even the pontifex would not escape oblivion."

The sound of these ghastly statements coming from such a precious little girl stunned me. Cardinal barely batted an eye as she continued, "The last one was the closest. I unleashed the strongest of all sacred arts attacks, and the torrent of lightning blasted Administrator's vast life amount down to just a single digit. Then the main process regained control of the body...and at that point, anything less than death was effectively nothing. Within moments, she had restored all health with the right commands. And that incident was enough for Administrator to feel threatened by her unconscious subprocess at last. When she realized that my moments of control came during instances of fluctlight conflict—meaning, mental instability—she used a preposterous means to lock me up for good."

"Preposterous...?"

"From her birth until she was chosen to serve Stacia, Administrator had been human. She had enough emotion to find flowers beautiful and music enjoyable. That humane side of her from childhood had been relegated to deep in her soul ever since she became the ultimate ruler of this world. She determined that the infinitesimal unrest she felt during spontaneous events was caused by that emotion of hers. So she used the admin commands for directly manipulating lightcube fluctlights to eliminate her own emotional circuits."

"Uh...when you say eliminate her circuits, you mean she destroyed part of her own soul?" I asked, chilled.

Cardinal nodded, frowning.

"B-but that's crazy," I continued. "It sounds way more dangerous than even that fluctlight copying experiment you described..."

"She did not just pop right into her soul and do it, of course. It was the Administrator's style to be aggravatingly cautious in matters like this. Have you noticed that the people of this world have hidden parameters that are not displayed on their Stacia Windows?"

"Y-yes, I suspected as much...I've seen several people whose appearance didn't reflect their strength and agility...," I replied, thinking of Sortiliena, whom I'd served as a page for my year in the academy. She was so slender that she seemed fragile, yet she'd bowled me over multiple times when we clashed.

And yet this little girl, who looked far weaker than her, possessed a bottomless well of imposing presence and power. Her hat bobbed. "Yes. Among those hidden parameters is a value called the *violation index*. It is a numerical representation of each civilian's degree of obedience to the law as measured through their statements and actions. It was probably created for outside observers to easier monitor the in-simulation subjects... but Administrator quickly discovered that she could utilize this value to sniff out those people who were skeptical of her Taboo Index. To her perfect world, these people were like bacteria sneaking into a sterilized clean room. She wanted to exterminate them all at once, but she could not break the rule forbidding murder that her parents had impressed upon her as a small child. So Administrator attempted a horrifying experiment that would not kill those with a high violation index but still render them harmless…"

"And…that's the punishment crueler than death that you mentioned?"

"Indeed. As experimental subjects for her fluctlight-manipulation rituals, she chose people with a high violation index. What information was stored where on the lightcube? Which spot should you tinker with to cause loss of memory, loss of emotion, loss of thought? Hideous, inhuman experiments that even the observers in the outside world hesitated to attempt," she said, ending in a whisper.

Goose bumps rose on my arms.

Her face looked downcast, and her voice was quiet, stifled. "…Most of those used for the original experiments did not emerge with any personality to speak of. They merely breathed, nothing more. Administrator froze their bodies and life and stored them in the cathedral. Over time, she gained experience in manipulating fluctlights, and when she was ready to lock out her own emotional side to keep me away, she had learned plenty after copious tests on the people she'd brought to the tower. At the time, she was about a hundred years old."

"…Was she successful?"

"You could say she was. It didn't eliminate all her emotions, but the experiment did manage to remove fear, shock, and anger—feelings that might cause momentary impulses. Since then, Administrator has never been shaken by any situation, no matter what. She is like a god…no, like a machine. A being that maintains the world, keeps it stable, keeps it stagnant…I was banished to a distant corner of her soul, never to reappear on the surface. Until the moment she turned one hundred and fifty, when her fluctlight hit its maximum storage and she took over the soul of that poor girl."

"But…based on everything you've told me, the soul that Administrator put into that furniture-maker's daughter was just a copy, right? So the emotions of that soul should've been limited from the start...How were you able to rise to the surface at that moment?" I asked. Cardinal's eyes traveled somewhere distant, likely through the mind-numbing span of two hundred years of time.

Very faintly, she said, "My vocabulary...does not have the words to properly describe that moment...the horrifying eeriness of it all...Administrator summoned the furniture-maker's girl to the top floor of the cathedral and attempted the Synthesis Ritual on her, to overwrite her soul. It worked successfully. The girl's unnecessary memories were deleted, replaced by a compressed version of Administrator's—of Quinella's—mind. Her original plan, once she was sure it had been successful, was for the maxed-out Quinella to eliminate her own soul...However..."

Cardinal's cheeks, which were normally a healthy red, were now as white as paper, I noticed. Despite her claim that she had no emotions, it seemed she was grappling with a deep, inescapable fear right then.

"...However, when the replication was complete and both bodies opened their eyes at close range...there was a kind of tremendous shock. I suppose...it was something like a sense of aversion, of wrongness...that, impossibly, there were two of the exact same person in existence. I...no, we...stared at each other, then felt an abrupt surge of hostility. Something that said the other could not be allowed to exist...It was more than an emotion—it was an impulse...something like a fundamental rule that must be acknowledged in the deepest core of the sentient mind. If that situation were allowed to continue, I daresay that both our souls would have obliterated themselves in their inability to withstand the truth. But...in the end, that did not happen, as disappointed as I am to admit it. The fluctlight copied onto the furniture-maker's daughter was the first to shatter, and in that instant, I seized control as the sub-personality. Thus, we recognized each other as Administrator in Quinella's body and the Cardinal subprocess in the girl's body. Our souls stopped collapsing and stabilized."

Soul collapse.

This phrase seemed to perfectly match the stomach-churning, eerie experience I'd witnessed just two nights before. I crossed swords with Raios Antinous, first-seat elite disciple at Swordcraft Academy, and severed both his hands with a Serlut-style Ring Vortex. This could easily be fatal in the real world, but he would have survived in the Underworld if given prompt treatment. I moved to clamp down the wounds to stop the bleeding and preserve his life—his numerical hit points, as this world defined them.

But before I could help him, Raios let out a horrifying scream, fell to the floor, and perished. Blood still flowed from his stumps, meaning that his life wasn't yet at zero. Raios had died of some cause that was not the elimination of his life value.

He had been placed in a quandary where he could either protect his life or uphold the Taboo Index, but not both. Unable to choose, he apparently got stuck in an infinite mental loop, until his very soul self-destructed.

I imagined that what happened to Quinella when faced with her copy was fundamentally the same. The terror of knowing that someone else possessed all your memories and thought the exact same way must have been beyond imagination.

For the first few days after I awoke in the forest near Rulid, I was unable to determine beyond a doubt that I was the real Kazuto Kirigaya and not just an artificial fluctlight copied from my mind. Until the moment Selka the church girl helped me confirm I could defy the ultimate set of laws in this land, I had feared that possibility.

What if my mind was set adrift in infinite darkness and I heard my own familiar voice say, "You're a replica of me. An experimental test subject that can be erased with the press of a key." How shocking, how confusing, how terrifying that would be...

"Do you understand everything so far?" The voice across the table sounded like a wizened instructor. I looked up, realizing that I'd been busy frying my brain, and made a vague gesture.

"Um…yeah, kind of…"

"I am finally about to get to the part of my lesson most relevant to you. I cannot have you struggling to keep up."

"The most relevant part? Oh…right. I still haven't heard what you actually want me to do."

"Yes. I have been waiting for two hundred years for the chance to explain this to you…So, I was at the point where I split off from Administrator," Cardinal said, twirling the empty teacup in her hands. "At last, I had gained a body of flesh all my own. Technically, it belonged to a poor girl who'd been training to be a nun… but she vanished entirely in the moment that her lightcube's data were overwritten. Once I was born through that cruel ritual and unexpected accident, I stared at Administrator for point-three seconds before I finally took the action that needed to be taken. I attempted to erase her with the highest level of sacred arts. I was a perfect copy of Administrator, so I had the same level of system access. If I struck first, I calculated that even if she fought back with a spell of the same level, I could consume all her life points before the spatial resources went dry. My first attack landed, and things went as I expected after that. The top floor of Central Cathedral was racked by thunder and lightning, gales of wind, and flames and ice blades as our respective life points steadily dropped from the damage. We were losing life at exactly the same pace…meaning that since I had drawn first blood, I should have emerged victorious in the end."

I tried to imagine a battle between god and god, and shivered. The only attacking sacred arts I knew were the very simple kinds I'd used in battle against Eldrie, simple manifestations of the element in question. They were less powerful than a sword swing, better for covering fire or blinding a target. Using them to wipe out another person's life…?

"Huh? Hang on. You just said that Administrator couldn't commit murder. Shouldn't that limitation also apply to you, too, since you're her copy? How were you able to attack each other?"

Cardinal looked slightly peeved that she'd been interrupted at a particularly dramatic part of her story, but she obliged anyway.

"Ah...that is a good question. As you said, Administrator was not bound by the Taboo Index of her own creation, but she could not break the rule against killing from Quinella's childhood. Even after years and years of study, I have not discovered the reason that we artificial fluctlights are totally unable to disobey our higher orders...but this phenomenon is not as absolute as you might believe."

"...Meaning...?"

"For example..."

Cardinal moved her right hand, holding the teacup, over the table. But rather than set it on the saucer, she made to set it down on an empty bit of tablecloth—except that her arm paused right before it made contact.

"I cannot lower the cup any farther than this."

"Huh?" I gaped.

She scowled and explained, "When I was young, my mother—Quinella's mother, I mean—taught me that a teacup must be placed on the saucer. It was a very minor rule, but one that still holds power. The only truly great crime was murder, but there are seventeen other taboos still active, including such silly rules as this one. I cannot lower my arm any farther than this, and if I try, I will feel a terrible pain within my right eye."

"...Right...eye..."

"But even this is significantly different from what ordinary civilians feel. They cannot fathom the idea of placing the cup anywhere but the saucer in the first place. In other words, they are ignorant of the fact that these absolute boundaries are shaping their minds. Of course, such ignorance can be bliss..."

Cardinal put on a wry, self-deprecating grimace that was completely at odds with her childlike appearance—a sign that she recognized her artificial roots. She returned her arm to its usual position.

"Now, Kirito...does this look like a teacup to you?"

"Eh?" I squawked, staring at the empty cup in Cardinal's hand. It was white porcelain, with simple curves and a plain handle. Aside from a single navy blue line around the rim, there was no decoration.

"Uh...sure, it looks like a teacup. I mean, it had tea in it..."

"Aha. And how about now?"

She tapped the rim of the cup with her free hand. Once again, liquid filled the cup from the base, sending up a column of white steam. But the smell was different this time—my nose twitched. It was too rich and tangy to be tea. No, this was cream of corn soup.

Cardinal tilted the cup so that I could crane my neck and see inside. As I expected, the contents were thick and pale yellow. There was even a crispy crouton floating in it.

"C-corn soup! Thanks, I was just feeling hungry..."

"I'm not asking you what's in it, fool! What is the container?"

"Err...well...I mean..."

The cup hadn't changed in the least since the previous moment. But now that she mentioned it, it did seem a little too simple, a little too big, a little too thick to be a typical teacup.

"Uh...a soup cup?" I guessed. Cardinal grinned and nodded.

"Yes. Now it is a soup cup. There is soup in it."

And to my shock, she set down the cup right on the tablecloth with a little thump.

"Wha...?!"

"See? In a sense, the taboos inflicted upon artificial fluctlights are very soft and vague. Simply changing one's subjective viewpoint makes them easy to overturn."

"..."

Stunned, I revisited the scene in the dorm from two days before. The very moment I had burst into the bedroom, Raios was about to bring his sword down on the prostrate Eugeo. If I hadn't blocked it with my weapon, he would certainly have cut Eugeo's head from his shoulders.

Obviously, killing was the greatest of taboos. But to Raios in that moment, Eugeo was not a fellow human being but a criminal guilty of violating the Taboo Index. By viewing the situation in that light, he easily circumvented that soul-etched command.

Eventually, I heard a creak from the back of the other chair at the table. Cardinal had lifted her tea/soup cup to her lips. The meat bun and sandwich I'd eaten many minutes ago had already been converted to life points, and my empty stomach clenched up.

"...May I have some of that?"

"You are a greedy fellow, aren't you? Give me your cup," she said, exasperated. She leaned over to the cup I was holding out and tapped on the rim. The empty receptacle filled up with that fragrant creamy yellow liquid.

I drew it back quickly, blew on the steam, and then sipped it. A rich, familiar taste filled my mouth, and I closed my eyes to savor it. The Underworld had a soup with a similar flavor, but it had been two years since I had an honest-to-God cream of corn soup.

I took another sip or two and exhaled with satisfaction, and Cardinal took that as her cue to continue.

"Now, as I just demonstrated, a simple change of perspective can allow me to overturn the taboos that bind me. We—Administrator and I—did not view each other as humans in that moment of battle. To me, she was a broken system that threatened the world, and to her, I was an annoying virus that could not be deleted...We spared no effort to eliminate the other's life, using sacred arts of the maximum power possible. In just two or three more blows, I would have destroyed Administrator or, at the very least, ensured our mutual death."

Her lips pursed, reliving the memories of regret and frustration. "But...but then, right at the end, that devious witch recalled the one definitive difference between us."

"Definitive difference...? But I thought the only thing that separated you two was your appearances. You had the same system access level and knew all the same commands, right?"

"Indeed. While we fought with sacred arts, it was clear that I would win in the end, thanks to my successful initiative. And so…she abandoned her spells. She converted one of the many high-priority objects in the chamber into a weapon, and then designated the very space where we fought as an invalid address for system commands."

"B-but…wouldn't she be unable to undo the order?"

"Exactly. Not unless she left that space. When she started chanting the command to generate a weapon, I realized what she was up to. But there was nothing I could do. Once I was unable to make a command, I could not undo it, either…So I was forced to join her in generating a weapon and attempted to finish her off with physical damage."

Cardinal paused, then lifted the staff leaning against the table. She extended it toward me without a word, and, surprised, I reached out to take it. The instant I was the one supporting it, the unbelievable weight yanked at my arm, and it took both hands to set the fragile-looking stick down on the table. The staff thudded loudly on the surface, clearly possessing a priority level at least as high as my sword or Eugeo's.

"I see…so not only is your sacred arts level godly, but so is your weapon-equipping level," I noted, rubbing my wrist. Cardinal shrugged, as if this was obvious.

"Administrator didn't just copy her memory and thought processes but all her authority levels, life points, and everything else. The sword she fashioned and my staff there were completely equal in strength. Even without sacred arts, I still believed that I would win a physical battle in the end. But once I held my staff, I realized Administrator's plan at last, and the definitive quality that separates us…"

"You keep mentioning that. What is it?"

"It's quite simple. Just look at my body."

She opened the front of her thick robe to reveal a white blouse, black pants, and white high socks. In stark contrast to her ancient scholar's manner, she had the fragile, weak body of a little girl.

I looked away on instinct, sensing that I had just seen something I wasn't meant to view, and asked, "What is it…about your body…?"

She folded the robe closed again and growled, "How dense can you be? Imagine that your mind was put in this body. Your eye level and arm's reach would be totally different. Do you think you could use your sword the same way you did before?"

"…Oh…"

"Until that point, I had been in Quinella's body, which was very tall for a woman. During our exchanges of sacred arts attacks, I hadn't noticed it much…but it wasn't until I held my staff and prepared to intercept her attack that I realized what a desperate situation I'd been placed in."

Now that I saw it from her perspective, I recognized the truth of that statement. Among the many VRMMOs out there, choosing an avatar with a vastly different size profile from your real body was disorienting, and it took a considerable amount of time and experience before close-quarters combat felt comfortable again.

"…So what *is* the height difference between you and Administrator, anyway…?"

"At least a foot and a half. I can still picture her expression, the way she looked down on me and smiled. Our battle resumed just after that, but within two or three strikes, I had to admit that my chances for victory were all but gone…"

"And…then what happened?"

I was here talking to her now, so obviously she'd somehow pulled through, but I held my breath like the story was unfolding before my eyes.

"Administrator had the advantage, but she made one simple mistake. If she had actually locked the doorway before she nullified all system commands within the chamber, she would have easily slaughtered me then and there. With my lack of human emotions"—I chose not to point out that she looked visibly upset right now—"I determined that immediate escape was necessary and darted for the door like a rabbit. With each scrape from Administrator's sword to my back, I felt my life depleting…"

"Wow…that's scary…"

"You may find yourself in the same situation, after two years and two months of drooling over every woman you've met."

"I…I wasn't drooling!" I protested, rubbing my mouth at this unexpected assault on my character. "W-wait, hang on. Two years and two months…? You haven't been watching me all along, have you?"

"Of course I have. Yes, it was only twenty-six months out of my two centuries, but even then, it was far longer than I expected."

"Wha…?"

I was stunned. Every single thing I'd done on the way here had been observed by this little sage? I didn't think much of it would be worthy of embarrassment, but I also couldn't be sure that none of it was. I didn't have time now to go back and reflect on two-plus years of memories…or so I told myself.

"W-well, we can get back to that later. Anyway…how did you escape from the Administrator?"

"Hmph. Well, I escaped out of her chamber door on the top floor of Central Cathedral, thus restoring my access to sacred arts, but it did not change the situation. If I tried to attack with spells again, she could just label the hallway a no-commands zone as well. The only thing that changed was that my method of escape went from running to flight. In order to regroup and recover, I had to flee to a place where her attacks could not reach me."

"Yeah, but…she's literally the administrator of this entire world, right? Can there *be* a place that she can't get to?"

"Being the administrator of the game might make her a god in a sense, but she is not truly omnipotent. There are just two places in this world that she cannot go."

"Two…?"

"One is the place beyond the End Mountains…the Dark Territory, as the humans call it. The other is the Great Library, where we are now. In fact, this library is a space she created herself, a kind of external memory storage when she learned that there was a limit to her memory. It contains all the system commands and a vast amount of data relating to the Underworld. Therefore, she decided that no person aside from her should ever be allowed to set foot in it. Administrator fashioned it so that despite being located within the cathedral tower, it occupies its own isolated space, with no connection outward. There is only one doorway in, and only she—no, only she *and I* know the command to get through."

"Aha…," I murmured, looking around the Great Library again, with its countless aisles, staircases, and bookshelves. The rounded walls looked like nothing but unbroken brick patterns. "Then, beyond that wall is…"

"Nothing. The wall itself is indestructible, but even if you could tear it down, you would find only an empty void beyond."

Briefly, I wondered what would happen if you jumped into that void. Then I shook my head and asked, "Is that door you mentioned the thing we passed through to get here from the rose garden?"

"No, that is something I created far later. Until two hundred years ago, there was a large set of double doors in the center of the lowest level. During my desperate flight from Administrator, I chanted the spell to call forth that door—and even I had to start over twice. Once I finished the command at last, the door appeared at the end of the hallway, and I plunged through it, then closed and locked it."

"Locked it? But if you and Administrator had the same authority level, couldn't she just open it right after you?"

"Indeed. But fortunately for me, while locking the library door from the inside is as simple as turning a key, it requires a very long and tedious unlocking art from the outside. Through the door, I could hear Administrator's cold and hateful voice chanting the unlocking command while I was busy casting a new spell of my own. I saw the lock turning counterclockwise just at the moment I finished my own chant..."

Cardinal clutched herself, reliving the memory. It was a two-hundred-year-old event, and yet I felt a chill just imagining it. I finished the last of the corn soup and summoned up the courage to ask, "Were you chanting a spell...to destroy the door?"

"Precisely. I obliterated the great doors, the only entrance to the cathedral's Great Library. In that instant, this place became unmoored from the outside world...thus allowing me to escape Administrator's wrath."

"...And why didn't she just create another door...?"

"What did I tell you earlier? Administrator first created the entire library, including the door, and then ripped it loose from the physical space of the cathedral. The spatial coordinates of this place as registered with the system are constantly switching through unused space at random. Unless she can precisely predict the correct numbers, it is impossible to breach this place from the outside."

"I see...but the coordinates of Central Cathedral *are* fixed, so you can open a hallway from here to the outside."

"Exactly. But because any door I create, once opened, will immediately be sniffed out by Administrator's agents, I cannot use them twice. Just like what happened with the rose garden door I used to scoop up you and Eugeo."

"Th-thanks for that...," I said, bowing. The little sage chuckled, then looked up to the domed ceiling of the library. She narrowed her eyes and said, in careful reflection, "...I fought against an error that needed correcting, and I lost. I ran in disgrace to this hiding place...and I have spent the two centuries since on observation and consideration..."

"...Two centuries..."

But of course, I'd only lived seventeen and a half years in the real world, plus two years of accelerated time in the Underworld. With less than twenty under my belt, it was impossible for me to fathom that length of time. I could only imagine the vague expanse of history.

The little girl sitting across from me had lived through that virtually infinite span, surrounded by nothing but silent mounds of books in this vast library, without even a mouse to interact with, much less another person. It was a totally unfathomable isolation from the world, something the word *solitary* didn't even begin to describe. If I had been in the same situation, I would never have lasted two centuries. I would have opened the door to the outside, even knowing it meant certain oblivion.

But actually, that made me think of something...

"Wait, Cardinal...What about that stuff you were saying about the one-hundred-and-fifty-year life span of the fluctlight? It was that very limit that caused Administrator to copy her own soul... So how have you managed the two hundred years since that split?"

"A very reasonable question," Cardinal said, leisurely lowering her emptied cup to the table. "Administrator might have chosen which parts of her she was going to copy to my fluctlight, but it did not leave room for such an enormous memory extension. So the first thing I did after I confirmed I was safe in the library was to undertake the process of arranging my memories."

"A-arranging...?"

"Yes. Direct-editing a file without a backup, according to the analogy I made earlier. If I committed a single mistake in the process, my consciousness would have melted within the light-cube, I daresay."

"So, uh...you're saying that even isolated within this Great Library, you still have the user authority to modify the Light-cube Cluster in the real world? Couldn't you access Administrator's fluctlight somehow and find a way to blow up her soul or whatever...?"

"Then the inverse would be true as well. But sadly—or fortunately—any kind of sacred art that causes a change in the status of an external target, as a fundamental rule, requires either physical contact or visual confirmation of the target unit or object. Regardless of any 'casting range,' in fact. It is why Administrator had to bring that furniture-maker's daughter up to the cathedral, and why she needed to have you and Eugeo brought to the Church."

I felt an involuntary shiver. If our reckless prison escape hadn't been successful, who knows what kind of torture we'd have suffered during the interrogation.

"In other words, while isolated inside the library like this, I had no means of attacking Administrator's fluctlight, but it also meant I had successfully escaped her wrath," Cardinal said, her long eyelashes lowered. "Organizing my own soul...was truly a horrifying task. A single command simply obliterates a memory that might have been vivid right until the moment of deletion. But I had to do it. Under the circumstances, I could easily imagine that it would take an unfathomable length of time to completely eradicate Administrator. Ultimately, I was able to remove all my memories as Quinella and ninety-seven percent from the moment I became Administrator..."

"B-but...that's almost all your memory, period!"

"Correct. That long, long story of Quinella I told you was not actually from my own experience but a written record I left before deleting it from my mind. I cannot recall the faces of the parents who gave birth to me. Or the warmth of the bed I slept in or the flavor of my favorite sweetbread...Remember what I told you? I have no human emotion. I have erased virtually all my memories and sentiments, leaving only a program that follows a desperate soul-etched order to stop the out-of-control main process. That is all I am."

"..."

And yet, in Cardinal's downcast smile, I saw an unspeakable loneliness. I wanted to tell her that she wasn't a program, that she must have the same emotions as me and other people, but I couldn't put it into words.

She looked up into my eyes, grinned again, and resumed speaking. "...After the process of self-deleting my memories, I had secured a healthy amount of fluctlight space. With the vast amount of time ahead, I began to work on a plan that would allow me to strike down Administrator in one righteous blow and avenge my miserable defeat. At first, I intended to catch her by surprise in direct combat. She cannot connect to this library from the outside, but as you now know, the reverse is possible. There is a range limit to the command to create a door, which means that I can place it anywhere from Central Cathedral gardens to the middle floors. On rare occasions, she does visit the lower floors, so I could have taken advantage of that to open a door and ambush her. Plus, to my surprise, I had adjusted to this body's control quickly."

"...I see. If you could guarantee the initiative, it seems worth trying...but it's still a huge gamble, right? You'd expect Administrator to make arrangements of her own..."

Ambushes were surprisingly hard to pull off when the target already anticipated a possible attack. I'd been through both sides of ambushes with orange players in *SAO*, and in virtually every case, an ambush from a "perfect" ambush location would fail to take a wary target by surprise. Cardinal grimaced and nodded.

"Quinella was always skilled at identifying others' weaknesses, even before she declared herself pontifex. In the same way she promptly isolated my size disadvantage in our separation battle, she identified an advantage she possessed in a different set of circumstances and made use of it."

"But...don't you essentially have the same attack and defense values? And, uh, mental capabilities. How could she have an advantage?"

"I don't like the way you say that...but you are correct." She snorted. "She and I are essentially identical in terms of single combat. But only in a one-on-one battle."

"One-on-one...Ohhh, I get it."

"Indeed. I am a solitary warrior hiding in my refuge, while she rules over the largest organization in the world...But I shall explain events in order. After she created me and was driven to the brink of death for it, Administrator recognized the great danger of copying her own fluctlight. Yet she was still faced with the peril of her logic circuits collapsing under the weight of her overflowing memories. She had to do something, but unlike me, she was not able to delve into the risky experiment of editing her memories directly. Instead, she aimed for a compromise. She chose to delete a relatively safe, surface-level category of memories to create a minimal sliver of free space, and then aggressively pruned any newly recorded information after that."

"Pruned...? But won't the memories build up anyway, even over the span of a single day?"

"It depends on how you spend it. If you see, do, and think a lot, you will have a larger input. But if you stay entirely within your canopy bed, passing the time with your eyes closed, it is a different story, is it not?"

"Ugh...I couldn't handle it. I'd rather spend an entire day just swinging a sword over and over."

"I am well acquainted with your restlessness at this point."

I had no comeback to this. If, for whatever reason, Cardinal had been monitoring my activity all along, she would already know about my habit of wandering away from Eugeo for a stroll whenever I had the free time.

The sage let her wry little grin fade before resuming her story. "But unlike you, Administrator is not bound by feelings such as boredom or ennui. If needed, she would stay in a prone position for days or even weeks at a time. All the while, drifting in a half-sleeping state through her fond memories leading up to ruling the world..."

"But she's the top boss of the Axiom Church, right? Doesn't she have stuff to do for that? Managing things, giving speeches, and the like?"

"She did, up to a point. She would accept a visit from the four emperors at the Great Solemnity to start the year, plus periodic visits to the middle and lower floors to ensure that the world was being controlled the way she wanted. Each and every time, she was on guard for an ambush from me. So Administrator played a new hand. She delegated the majority of her duties and arranged for powerful, loyal servants who would help protect her..."

"So that's the advantage she had as the head of a huge ruling force, as opposed to you being on your own...But wouldn't that just create more variables for her to have to deal with? If her group of guards was capable of fighting off the one with as much strength as her, how would she control it if they decided to turn on her?" I wondered.

Cardinal shrugged, repeating, "What did I say? Absolute loyalty."

"Look, I know people can't disobey orders from above, but you already showed me that those aren't absolute. What if the guards somehow decided that their pontifex was actually acting on behalf of the Dark Territory...?"

"Naturally, she was aware that the possibility of that was greater than zero. She had been experimenting on people with a high violation index, after all. Blind obedience is not the same as loyalty...And even if those guards truly swore to protect her with the utmost faith, she would not believe it. Remember, she was betrayed by her own copy," Cardinal said with a devilish grin. "If she was going to give them equal authority and equipment, she needed a guarantee that they would not disobey her under any circumstances. How does one do that? Simple: alter their fluct-lights to make it so."

"...Uh...what?"

"She completed the complex, lengthy commands to achieve this end. In other words, Synthesis Ritual."

"That's...fusing memories to a soul, right?"

"Yes. And she had plenty of high-quality subjects with powerful souls to use. All those individuals with the high violation index values who she experimented upon and then froze were also universally gifted with significant talent…In fact, you might say it was their excellent intellect and physique that led them to doubt the power of the Taboo Index and Axiom Church in the first place…Among those she captured first was an unparalleled swordsman who drifted to the frontier with his companions out of distaste for the Church's rule and founded his own village. He was arrested when he attempted to cross the End Mountains that separate the human world from the Dark Territory, and Administrator chose him to be the first of her faithful servants."

For some reason, this story tickled at my memory, though I couldn't recall where I'd heard it. Before I could remember, Cardinal continued, "The majority of the swordsman's memory was damaged from the experiments, but that was actually to Administrator's benefit—she didn't want his precapture memories interfering. So she created an object called a Piety Module that forces absolute servitude—it looks like a purple prism about this big…"

She held out her fingers about four inches apart. The instant I could picture it in my head, every hair on my body stood on end. I had seen one of them. Just hours ago, in fact.

"…The Synthesis Ritual involves embedding the prism into the center of the target's forehead. This fuses the memory-stripped soul with the generated memories and prime directive, thus creating a brand-new persona. A superwarrior that is absolutely loyal to the Church and Administrator, acting only to uphold the status quo of the world…When the ritual was successful and her subject awoke, she gave him the title of Integrity Knight, symbolizing his role in correcting chaos, furthering the Church's rule, and upholding the integrity of the world order. If you climb the cathedral, you and Eugeo may very well come across the oldest of the knights. You ought to know his name."

She looked solemnly into my eyes and announced, "The name of the knight is…Bercouli Synthesis One."

"…No. No, no, no, that can't be right," I blurted before Cardinal's mouth had even closed.

Bercouli.

The legendary hero Eugeo had told me about, his face shining with awe and reverence. He was one of the original pioneers of Rulid, an explorer of the End Mountains, and the fearless adventurer who attempted to steal the Blue Rose Sword from the white dragon that protected the human realm.

Eugeo hadn't known anything about Bercouli's final years. I just imagined that he had lived in Rulid until he was old—but never guessed that he'd been abducted by Administrator and turned into the original Integrity Knight.

"Um, Cardinal…you realize that Eugeo and I had to team up against Eldrie Synthesis Thirty-One—meaning the thirty-first of the series—and barely held our own, right? There's no way we could tackle the first one and win."

But the sage merely shrugged off my protest. "You cannot afford to quake at the idea of Bercouli alone. As you just mentioned, there are thirty-one knights in total now."

"For there being so many, I sure haven't seen much of them. Since coming to Centoria, I've only even seen an Integrity Knight flying on their dragon once, at night."

"Naturally. The duty of the knights is to protect the End Mountains. The only time they appear in the city is when someone commits a major violation of the Taboo Index, and that doesn't happen even once a decade. Not even nobles or emperors witness Integrity Knights regularly, much less the common folk…In fact, you might say their isolation is intentional…"

"Hmm…So does that mean the majority of the other thirty knights are in the mountains?" I asked, clinging to faint hope, but Cardinal dashed it at once.

"Not the majority. At present, the awakened knights in the cathedral number at least twelve or thirteen. If you and Eugeo are to accomplish your individual goals, you must expect to defeat them all on the way to the top of the tower."

"Must expect to, huh…?"

I sank into my chair and exhaled. In RPG terms, it felt like I was about to charge into the final dungeon woefully underleveled and poorly equipped. It was true that I'd journeyed all this way to reach the top of Central Cathedral and make contact with someone in the real world, but even this close to my goal, I was at an overwhelming disadvantage against the Integrity Knights.

I looked down at my chest without comment. Thanks to Cardinal's magical meat buns, the wounds I suffered from Eldrie's Perfect Weapon Control were totally healed, but the lingering sensation of that tingling pain still remained.

If the Integrity Knights ahead were stronger than Eldrie, our chances of solving this in the orthodox way were extremely slim...and then I recalled that strange phenomenon that happened at the end of the battle in the rose garden.

When Eugeo had told the knight about his past and his mother's name, the knight had suddenly fallen to his knees in pain. While he was barely conscious, a translucent purple prism, glowing brightly, had emerged from his forehead. That must have been the Piety Module that Cardinal was just talking about. It controlled the knights' egos and memories, forcing them to be perfectly loyal to the pontifex.

But was the effect really as irreversible as Cardinal claimed? Just hearing his mother's name caused Eldrie's module to begin ejecting—or so it seemed. If the same effect happened with other knights, then that meant there was a way outside of crossing swords with them, and it made possible Eugeo's dream of turning Integrity Knight Alice back to regular Alice.

Then I heard Cardinal say, "My story is nearly over. Shall I continue?"

"...Oh, yeah. Please."

"Good. By creating a number of Integrity Knights, starting with Bercouli, Administrator had vastly decreased my chances of a successful ambush. The knights had excellent attack and defense skills, if not quite as high as Administrator, enough that even I could not eliminate them instantly. It forced me to confront the reality that my battle with her would last an unfathomably long time..."

It seemed that Cardinal's long, long story was reaching its conclusion. I straightened up in my chair and focused on the little sage's sonorous voice.

"With this change in the situation, it became clear that I would need an accomplice. But naturally, there are few who will willingly choose to help one battle against the absolute ruler of the world. Such a person would need a high enough violation index to break any taboo, as well as enough combat or sacred arts ability to counteract the Integrity Knights. So, dangerous as it was, I opened a door as distant as possible, cast spells of Sensory Sharing and such on the birds and bugs, then let them loose into the world..."

"Ha-ha...So those are your eyes and ears, huh? Is that how you were keeping tabs on me...?"

"Yes," she said with a smirk, reaching out. Her palm uplifted, she made a beckoning motion with her finger.

"Whoa!"

Abruptly, something very small leaped out of my hairline and onto Cardinal's palm. It was a black spider smaller than the tip of my pinkie. It spun around, looked up at me with four crimson eyes, and lifted its front right leg in what seemed like a salute.

"This is Charlotte. From the moment you and Eugeo left Rulid, she has been hiding in your hair, or your pocket, or the corner of your room, watching and listening to everything you two did. And apparently...doing more than that at times," Cardinal said. The spider tucked in its legs and seemed to shrink.

This cute little gesture suddenly caused me to recall the tug on my bangs pointing me in the right direction while we were running from the knight on the dragon. Perhaps that was the spider? In fact, that had happened more than once. After we left Rulid, during the tournament and garrison days in Zakkaria, even after starting at the academy in Centoria, I'd felt the same sensation at a number of crucial moments.

"...You mean that tugging sensation wasn't just my instincts talking to me? It was something literally pulling on my hair...?" I murmured, aghast. After all those memories, an extremely important one replayed in my mind. I bolted upright and leaned over the little black spider resting on Cardinal's palm.

"W-wait...When they cut down all my zephilia flowers, was it *you* trying to cheer me up...? The one who told me to believe in the zephilias' vitality and the other flowers' wishes..."

The voice in my memory had been a slightly older woman's. That would suggest that the black spider, as the name Charlotte suggested, had a female personality. Was that even possible? Could an insect have a soul—a fluctlight?

Charlotte answered my question with nothing but the gaze of her red eyes at first. Then the spider ran off Cardinal's palm and scurried across the tabletop, jumped to the nearby bookshelf, and disappeared.

Cardinal watched the little familiar go and said gently, "Charlotte is the oldest of the observation units that I cast spells on and unleashed into the world. Now her long, long mission is at an end. Because I froze the natural degradation of her life value, she's been working for over two hundred years..."

"...An observation unit...," I muttered, looking at the bookshelf Charlotte had vanished into. Her mission was simply to watch the actions of the two of us. But for the two years since leaving Rulid, Charlotte had been tugging on my hair and occasionally whispering her own advice to me. In a sense, she'd been a closer companion during this journey than even Eugeo.

Thank you, I whispered inside my mind, bowing toward the shelf. Then I looked back to Cardinal and said, "So basically... you've been stuck here in the Great Library, using familiars as your eyes and ears, searching for a possible human helper for over two centuries...?"

"Correct. I cannot view the violation index of individual humans from here. I have to keep an ear open for rumors of strange events, then send observers out to watch the people who were likely to have caused them. It is a very tedious, laborious process. More than once or twice, I have found promising people, only to see them hauled off and made into Integrity Knights. I have no emotions, but I've certainly learned enough about disappointment and patience. In fact…in the last decade, I've even begun understanding the concept of resignation," she said, her lips turned upward into a grin weighted with two centuries of life.

"While I sat back and watched the world, Administrator has been busy creating a proactive system of defense, securing powerful knights to do her bidding. In fact, that is the true purpose of the Four-Empire Unification Tournament that you and Eugeo sought to enter."

"…So the warrior who wins that tournament doesn't earn the glory of being promoted to Integrity Knight…"

"He or she is forced into becoming one. Their prior memories are placed behind a wall, and they become powerful, unthinking puppets for the pontifex's bidding. The families that produce Integrity Knights are given eye-popping payments and elite noble titles, so those lower nobles and merchants are happy to teach their children the sword, even if ultimate success means they will never see those sons or daughters again. The knights themselves are assigned to duties that will ensure they do not make accidental contact with those families. They are cut off from their pasts."

"…So that's what you meant when you said they were intentionally isolated…"

"Yes, I was speaking of this system. Of the thirty-one Integrity Knights, half were brought in for violating a taboo, and the other half were tournament champions. Eldrie Synthesis Thirty-One was the latter."

"I see…So that's how it works…," I said, exhaling gloomily.

So it was actually a good thing that neither Sortiliena, the student I served as page, or Eugeo's Golgorosso had been triumphant at this year's tourney. If Sortiliena had beaten Eldrie and gone on to win, then I would have encountered her in the rose garden as an Integrity Knight with her memory removed.

And there was more. If the incident with Raios and Humbert had never happened, and Eugeo and I had become school champions as we'd planned and then gone through the tournament and won—or if we'd never escaped those cells and had been taken in for questioning—then Eugeo could have ended up as the thirty-second Integrity Knight, even if my natural fluctlight kept me safe. We would have fallen right into a terrible trap. I shivered.

Cardinal quietly went on. "Over these two centuries, Administrator has steadily shored up her defenses, while I have nearly lost all hope. So yes, I began to wonder why I was even bothering..."

Her brown eyes stared up at the distant ceiling of the library. She blinked a few times, as though imagining warm sunlight streaming from the cold rock dome.

"...The world I saw through my observation units was beautiful and radiant. The children ran happily through the fields, girls blushed with romance, and mothers smiled at the babes in their arms with loving sentiment. If the furniture-maker's daughter whose body I possess had been allowed to grow like normal, she could have had all those things. She would have led a life untroubled by the workings of the world and, after sixty or seventy years, ended her life in bliss and satisfaction, surrounded by her family..."

Her voice stopped in a whisper, her eyes downcast. Cardinal's tiny body swayed a little—or at least, I imagined it did.

"...I cursed my prime directive, that drive to correct the main process that was etched into my soul. I realized I was an old crone, just before my natural death. All the sparkle of life had faded from me, like a wizened, weak tree, counting down the seconds until my life span was gone. Strangely enough, even my way of speaking began to reflect that view. As I spent my days

endlessly listening to the bustle of humanity through my familiars' ears, I pondered why the gods from the outside world would
abandon it to its fate under Administrator's heel...Stacia, Solus,
and Terraria are false gods created to suit the Axiom Church's
ends, but within the list of system commands, I spotted on multiple occasions the name of the true god: Rath. I learned that Rath
was a collection of gods...and I learned of their soulless approxi-
mation of a god, Cardinal—and that its two directives had been
burned into Administrator and me. The more I learned of the
underpinning ways of this world, the more mysteries appeared."

"W-w-wait a second," I pleaded, unable to keep up with her
story's momentum. "So...are you saying you were able to learn
that this is a simulation created by Rath, and that the original
Cardinal is a program with a main and a subprocess, using conjecture alone?"

"It is not so surprising. Between two hundred years of time and
the Cardinal System's built-in database, anyone would reach the
same conclusion."

"Database...? I see. So any non-Underworldian vocabulary
you've been using came from there."

"As well as the flavor of that corn soup you enjoyed. I expect
that your understanding of many of these terms is not the same
as mine...but at the very least, I believe my conjecture is accurate. The Underworld is far too incomplete to be the creation of
an all-powerful god, and given the way Administrator's hideous
corruption and tyranny are allowed to continue...there was only
one possibility: that Rath, the true god, does not seek the happiness of the Underworldians. On the contrary...this world exists
so they can observe how its people resist when they are slowly,
slowly drawn into a massive trap. You may not realize that in
recent years, the border regions of the human realms have been
increasingly inflicted with plagues, roving beasts, poor crops,
and other causes of premature death. These effects are caused
by a stress parameter that even Administrator is incapable of
altering."

"Stress...parameter? Actually, you mentioned something like that before, too. Something about a stress-test stage."

"Aye. Strictly speaking, the stress level rises from day to day... but the final phase of the test the database speaks of wouldn't be anything like a mere plague."

"So...what's going to happen...?"

"The forces that cradle the egg of the human realm will finally break. I'm sure you know what exists beyond that eggshell."

"The Dark Territory...?"

"Indeed. That land of darkness is a device created to inflict the ultimate agony on the people of this world. As I mentioned earlier, the denizens of the darkness—goblins, orcs, and so on—are like human beings, only their fluctlights have been given the prime directive of slaughter and pillage. Their societies are arranged by a power hierarchy where the spectrum of strength divides everything. Although primitive, their military is mighty. They have barely half the population of humankind, yet each individual is easily more powerful than a human being. Even now they wait outside the empire, looking forward to the day that they invade the territory of the Iums, as they call you, and wreak untold suffering. That day is close at hand."

"A military..."

The thought put more than a shiver down my back. The goblin captain I faced in the cave under the End Mountains two years ago was a true and mighty fighter. The thought of thousands upon thousands of them spilling into peaceful towns froze my innards. I shook my head rapidly in disbelief. My throat dry, I said, "...Th-there are many guardsmen and knights in the human lands...but they don't stand a chance. Especially not when the sword techniques here are focused on presentation..."

Cardinal promptly nodded in agreement. "As I expected... I suspect that in Rath's plans, the humans would have formed a military equal to the Dark Territory's by now—one nurtured on constant minor skirmishes with invading goblins, promoting healthy authority level growth in its fighters, with practical swordfighting and group strategy. But as you know, the situation is far from that ideal. Swordsmen pursue only the visual look of their styles without a single honest fight, and the nobles meant to lead any theoretical armies are pampered and self-obsessed. And all of this is a result of Administrator and her Integrity Knights."

"...What do you mean?"

"The Integrity Knights have the highest authority level and Divine Objects for weapons and armor. They are mighty indeed. Just eight of them are enough to fully patrol the End Mountains and drive off any invading bands of goblins. But that means that centuries have passed without any ordinary citizens being faced with the experience of battle. They lead lives of safe, comfortable stagnation, knowing nothing of the impending calamity that awaits them..."

"...Does Administrator know that the final phase of this stress test is about to begin?"

"I suspect that she does. But she is confident that she and her thirty knights alone will be enough to fight off the hordes of darkness. So confident, in fact, that she had the guardian dragons of the four cardinal directions slain; they should have been valuable allies in the fight, but she could not stand that they were not under her command. I have no doubt that your partner would be sad to hear that the legendary white dragon from his fond myths was actually killed by Bercouli himself, once reforged as an Integrity Knight."

"...Probably shouldn't let him know, then," I muttered with a sigh. I closed my eyes, envisioning the mountain of bones I saw in that cave, then looked up again. "So what's the score? When the forces of darkness invade, can Administrator and her Integrity Knights actually fight them off?"

"They cannot," she said bluntly. "The Integrity Knights are fierce warriors with many years of experience, but there are simply far too few of them. And Administrator's sacred arts are virtually godlike in their ability to disrupt the land, but as I said earlier, using them means putting herself within range of those foes. And while individually, they may fall far short of Administrator, there are as many users of system commands—what you might call dark magic, in this case—as stars in the sky. She might burn a hundred with lightning in one moment, and then be engulfed by a thousand fireballs the next. I do not know if that would actually kill her, but it is clear that she would eventually be forced to retreat to this tower."

"Um…wait a sec. Are you saying that…whether or not you and I beat Administrator, the ultimate fate of this world will be the same?" I asked, stunned. "That even if you regain the full powers of the Cardinal System, you won't actually be able to fight off the forces of darkness?"

She nodded gravely. "That is what I am saying. At this point, I have no means of preventing the invasion from the Dark Territory."

"…So…as long as you fulfill your purpose of deleting the malfunctioning main process—meaning Administrator—then… whatever happens to the world after that is none of your concern? Is that what you're saying…?" I rasped.

Cardinal pursed her lips, her eyes somewhat mournful as she stared through her little round glasses at me.

"…That may be correct." Her voice was so faint that it nearly blended into the minute sound of the lamp's flickering flame. "Indeed…if you look at it from the standpoint of the many souls that could be lost, my goal could be taken as an abandonment of the larger picture…But if you and I sit here and do nothing, then eventually…whether in a year or two or longer, the forces of darkness will invade. They will trample and burn fields and towns, and they will kill many people. It will be a hell that I haven't the words to describe—the ultimate expression of tragedy and cruelty. However…even if I recover all my powers and had the proper command to burn all those monsters into ash at once, I would not use it. They did not ask to be made monsters. As I said, you will not arrive at an answer even after a century of thinking. For you see…if Administrator had never come about here, and humanity had traced the path it was meant to follow, then at this time it would be the forces of man forming an army to invade the Dark Territory and commit unspeakable atrocities to their peoples, instead!"

Her soft voice got harder and harder until it cracked like a whip by the end. "In either case, the end of the world will involve great bloodshed. For that outcome was the design of the god Rath. And I…I cannot accept such a god. I will not accept this outcome under any circumstances. So when I learned that the arrival of the stress test was unavoidable, I landed on one simple conclusion. I would eliminate Administrator before that happened, restore my powers as the Cardinal System…and reduce the Human Empire, the Dark Territory—the entire Underworld—to nothingness."

"Reduce it…to nothingness…?" I repeated. Belatedly, my eyes bulged. "What does that mean…?"

"Just what it sounds like. I will delete all the fluctlights in that cradle of souls, the Lightcube Cluster. All of them, from both the human and dark side."

The determination on Cardinal's young face was so stark that I was unable to speak for several moments. Over time, the concrete facts of her final solution began to form a proper image in my head.

"So you're saying…that if the horrible agonizing deaths of many people is an inevitability, that it's better to put them all into a painless death before it reaches that point…?"

"Painless death…? No, that description is not accurate," Cardinal said, pausing briefly as if consulting an internal database. "Unlike you humans from the upper world, whose records are stored on a different medium than the lightcube, the souls of the Underworldians can be obliterated with an instantaneous command. They will simply vanish without a clue, and without any greater resistance than the flickering of a candle...which does not change the fact that it is still an act of murder..."

There were traces of deep resignation and powerlessness in her voice, as if this conclusion had been reached only after a very long period of consideration. "Of course, in ideal terms, the best outcome is for this world to continue free of Rath's meddling, fashioning its own history. After a few more centuries, perhaps even a peaceful accord between humanity and the Dark Territory is possible. But...I suppose you would know best of all that total independence from our god Rath is nothing but a pipe dream, wouldn't you?"

I bit my lip to think, surprised by the sudden question. I didn't know where in Japan the actual Lightcube Cluster that housed the Underworld was installed. But naturally, the cluster and all of its attendant machinery required a considerable amount of power to run. In that sense, true independence was functionally impossible.

And Rath wasn't running the Underworld as a charity. If my conjecture was accurate that Seijirou Kikuoka was part of the SDF, and deeply connected to the foundation of Rath, then the Defense Ministry must have a concrete goal in mind for it. Even if Cardinal recovered all her power, opened an external channel, and demanded independence for the Underworld, Rath would never accept it.

In fact, thinking about it now, even if I made it to the top of Central Cathedral, contacted Kikuoka, and begged him to preserve the current state of the Underworld, there was zero assurance that he would agree. To Rath, all these artificial fluctlights were test subjects. In fact, this particular Underworld was just one of a number of attempts.

Ultimately, if the artificial fluctlights wanted true freedom and independence, there was only one way to gain it—to take the fight to the people in the real world.

I had to stop myself from taking that line of thought any further—it was too frightening. I looked up at Cardinal and nodded, my neck stiff. "…You're right. It's not possible. This world is too dependent on the outside people and energy sources to ever be independent."

"Aye…we are like fish in a bucket, waiting to be fried in a pot. The best we can do is jump out now to certain death," Cardinal said, resigned. But I did not immediately support her conclusion.

"But…I'm not totally sure. Maybe you're right that vanishing instantaneously is a better answer than dying in agony. But I've become too involved with the people of this world to accept that as the only correct way."

The smiling faces of those who'd shown me kindness in Rulid and Centoria flashed through my mind's eye. I had no desire to see them slaughtered by the forces of the Dark Territory, of course, but would helping Cardinal delete everyone's souls really be the best choice?

I bit my lip, unable to accept this sudden, unwelcome thrust of reality. Gently, Cardinal said, "Kirito, if I am able to regain my full powers with your help, I can fulfill your wishes, up to a degree, before I eliminate the Underworld. If you single out the names of those you wish to save, I will freeze their fluctlights and save them, rather than wiping them clean. Then, after you escape to the real world, you can save the lightcubes that contain the souls in question. I doubt that ten would be impossible to set aside. It may not be the best possible solution for you, but it is better than you can expect."

"…!"

I sucked in a sharp breath, surprised by her answer. Was that even possible?

If lightcubes didn't need power to maintain their stored information, and you could safely extract them from the cluster without harming the contents, then the fluctlights themselves shouldn't ever degrade. It would take time, but if the Soul Translator tech became commonplace, I could theoretically thaw them out and see them again in the future.

The problem was the step before that. Could I really sneak multiple cubes out of the cluster at the very core of the Rath laboratory? According to Cardinal, they were two inches to a side. I couldn't hide several in my pockets at once. Even if I could carry them in a case, ten was about the limit of what I could extract.

So if I accepted her offer, that meant I had to choose the souls I wanted to save.

This wasn't like organizing save data on a game console. In a fundamental sense, the artificial fluctlights were just as human as I was. I would choose just ten in this entire world to save from certain death—and only because I got along with them. Did I have the right? Was I qualified to do such a thing?

"I...I..."

But I couldn't bring myself to say the word *can't*. Cardinal stared right through me, seeing all. The only thing I could produce was a pathetic complaint.

"Why did you single out me to be your coconspirator in fighting Administrator, anyway? Let me be clear: I have barely any unique advantages at all in this world. There are tons of people with better skill at sacred arts and swordfighting. In fact...even Eugeo. I bet that if we really fought head-to-head, I couldn't beat him anymore."

Once I was done with my feeble, passive defense, Cardinal shook her head in exasperation. She filled the cups on the table with cofil tea—or perhaps it was real coffee this time—and took a sip.

"...It was only twenty years ago that I realized that the stress test, the invasion from the Dark Territory, was inevitable. After that, I redoubled my efforts to find someone to fight on my behalf..."

I kept my further complaints to myself, sensing that her long, long story was finally reaching its conclusion.

"...But no matter how skilled in sacred arts and weapons the allies I could find were, there was one other huge obstacle to approaching Administrator that needed to be removed, aside from the Integrity Knights."

"…You mean there's more?"

"Indeed. I considered dozens of possible solutions as my search dragged on, but none was particularly practical…As time passed, and I realized we were in the prelude stages of the Dark Territory invasion, more and more advance parties began threatening the End Mountains—enough that the eight Integrity Knights tasked with protecting the area couldn't eliminate them all. Just when I was starting to consider giving up on forcibly restoring my authority and risking death in an attempt to convince Administrator instead…one of my familiars picked up on an extraordinary, impossible rumor spreading around the northern frontier lands."

"Impossible…?"

"It was the sort of event that had certainly never happened after Quinella became the Administrator. In order to prevent human settlement from spreading, she had set up massive impediments around the map…and one, a gigantic, resource-sucking tree with nearly limitless priority and durability, got chopped down by two boys."

"…Sounds familiar…"

"I sent my northern Norlangarth agent, Charlotte, to find those boys. She finally tracked them down just before they left the village. I had Charlotte hide in the hair of one of them, the sloppier one, so that I could seek the answer of how they eliminated a near-indestructible object…"

I wanted to respond to the "sloppy" comment, but then I remembered that Charlotte had been riding on my head for nearly two years without my realizing. I scowled and motioned for Cardinal to continue.

"I learned the direct reason promptly. The boy with the light brown hair possessed a sword, a Divine Object with few peers in the entire world. It was a legendary weapon only granted to heroes accepted by the world's dragon guardians, before they were slaughtered...But learning this only brought me fresh questions. Why would these children have such a high object control authority? It was an excitement I had not felt in years. I listened closely to their conversations, day and night. Nearly all of it was idiotic and pointless—"

"Geez, sorry."

"Shut up and listen. Eventually, in an inn along the way to Centoria, I finally understood the reason why. To my surprise, these two had vanquished a large-scale scouting party from the Dark Territory unaided, according to what they were saying. If true, that meant they each received half the authority advancement points that would normally be distributed among dozens of fighters. That explained how you were able to equip the weapon...but again, it raised more questions. How was it possible that two boys raised in a rural village without even a proper armed garrison managed to defeat the vastly more powerful goblin warriors of the Dark Territory?"

"Just to be clear, that was ninety percent bluff," I interjected. Cardinal made to scold me, then paused and seemed to accept it.

"Ah...yes, I suppose that would have been part of it. It took me quite a while before my doubts about this finally thawed. The black-haired boy—you, Kirito—seemed to be taking care with his statements out of concern for his partner, Eugeo. But when I saw you give extra food to a wild animal—a stray dog—I felt a shock like a bolt of lightning. I realized you were totally unbound by the Taboo Index..."

"...Did I do that...?"

"Several times. It would have caused great trouble if anyone had seen you. After that moment, I paid keen attention to everything you did and said, through Charlotte's eyes. Especially after you reached Centoria and passed through the gate of the North Centoria Imperial Swordcraft Academy. After a year of observation, I came to my answer at last. I knew you were not a soul born in this world and trapped in a lightcube…but a human being from the outside, the world where the god of creation Rath exists…"

"Then I suppose I've let you down. I don't have any of the administrative privileges or means to contact Rath that you'd expect…In fact, I don't even know what's going on in the outside world right now…," I said apologetically. Cardinal grinned and raised her index finger.

"I knew that from the start. If you had a higher system level than Administrator, you would not have suffered such a wound to defeat those goblins with a sword. Even I cannot surmise the reason you are in the Underworld in this state. Perhaps it is some kind of accident…or a data test with your memory and abilities limited. If the latter, it seems that you have paid a greater price than necessary."

"…Yeah, no kidding. I can't believe I'd agree to something like that," I muttered, recalling the pain in my shoulder where the goblin captain sliced me.

"But even still, you were the greatest opportunity I could have hoped for. Your existence itself would help me overcome that other great obstacle to fighting Administrator."

"And what is that obstacle?"

"The Synthesis Ritual requires an extremely lengthy spoken command and a vast amount of parameter adjustment. Including the preparatory stages, the entire process takes three full days."

Once again, this sudden topic change threw me for a loop. But Cardinal proceeded onward.

"Meaning that when it comes to ordinary combat, a sacred art that accesses the lightcube directly is not really a factor. In other words, there is no danger of having your soul taken over and turned into an Integrity Knight in the midst of battle. However, what if Administrator abandoned the idea of absorbing my chosen warrior and decided simply to destroy the soul altogether…? Without requiring stringent parameter adjustment, the command would become dramatically shorter. She might even finish the spell while her guards were still fighting. We can defend against direct life attacks with equipment and sacred arts. But if she attacks the fluctlight directly, there is no defense. This was a quandary that troubled me for many, many years."

"...An attack against the soul...That's pretty chilling..."

"Just so. Even the most skilled combatant is helpless if their memories are torn to pieces...Which means that you are the only one who can withstand such an attack, Kirito. Your Divine Object of the outside world, the device called the STL, transports your soul into the Underworld, and Administrator cannot harm it—there is no such command. Now do you see why I have awaited you so badly? It is the reason I have waited and worked so hard to install as many back doors as possible, to ensure that I could spirit you here into my library, in case you won the Unification Tournament or broke the Taboo Index and found yourself setting foot onto the Axiom Church's territory..."

At last, at long last, Cardinal had brought her story up to the present moment. She exhaled, her cheeks a bit reddened.

"...I see. So that's what this is about..."

Even at this late stage, I didn't know why I was here on a dive into the Underworld. If anything, my journey to the center of the world where I might find a way to contact Rath was as much to learn the reason as anything else.

But after hearing the story from this girl who had lived such an extremely long time, it was hard to argue against the idea that I was guided here by a kind of fate. The outcome of our battle against Administrator was uncertain, but there was a kind of divine voice telling me to do my utmost to help Cardinal and take ten people at maximum out to the real world with me...

But even before weighty concepts like fate came into the picture, I simply couldn't look into the eyes of a girl who had waited for two hundred years for this exact moment and tell her no. Over and over, she insisted she was an emotionless program, but over the course of her very long story, that seemed less and less true. Cardinal was another human being with her own emotions, just like me—even if she was bound by her great duty to correct the state of the world.

"What do you say, Kirito? I cannot force you...If you decide you cannot agree to my plan to wipe the world clean, I can send you and Eugeo out of a back door of your choosing. If so, and you find some way to defeat Administrator and achieve your goals, you might be fighting me next...but I suppose that is simply fate at work..."

And then, Cardinal gave me a dazzling, transparent smile, one that suited her visual age better than any expression I'd seen yet. I held my silence for a long, long time and then asked, "Cardinal...you said that your soul was a copy of Quinella's, right...?"

"Aye. That is absolutely correct."

"Then...you must have the blood of pure nobles, too—the genes that command you to pursue your own profit and desires. Why didn't you give all of this up and just flee for your life? You could go to some distant village, a place so far and insignificant that even Administrator couldn't find you, fall in love, get married, have children...and then grow old and die happy. Wasn't that your wish? Your blood should have ordered you to fulfill that desire, for these two hundred years. Why have you been waiting here, alone, resisting your command for all this time...?"

"You really are a fool." She grinned. "I told you. The Cardinal subprocess's reason for existence is carved into my soul. I have only one wish: to eliminate Administrator and restore normal function to the world. To me, there is no way to have a properly functioning world other than to wipe the slate clean. Therefore... therefore, I..."

She faltered, and I stared through her glasses at her eyes. Those burnt-brown irises were wavering, clearly holding in some sweep of emotion. When her lips moved again, they emitted a voice that was barely even audible.

"…No…that's wrong…I…I do have a desire…Something that I just had to know…for these two hundred long years…"

She closed her eyes, lifted her face, and stared right at me. She bit her lip in hesitation, folded her hands for several moments, then abruptly leaped to her feet.

"Kirito, stand up with me."

"Huh…?"

I got out of my seat. Once I was upright, Cardinal gazed at me, her back considerably arched. I wasn't that tall in the grand scheme of things, but there was a big difference between me and the girl, whose appearance was that of a ten-year-old.

Cardinal looked around, squinting, then put a foot on her chair and lifted herself up. When she had confirmed that we were at the same eye level, she nodded in satisfaction.

"Good. Come here, Kirito."

"…?"

I took a few steps until I was standing in front of Cardinal, still confused.

"Closer."

"What?"

"Just do it!"

I inched forward, despite my misgivings. When she told me to stop, our bangs were nearly brushing. A nervous sweat broke out on my skin as she stared into my eyes, then away.

"Raise your arms."

"…Like this?"

"Now make a circle with them in front."

"………"

Tentatively—and half expecting her to bash me with her staff as soon as I actually did what she told me—I circled my arms around Cardinal's back and touched my fingers together, making sure to leave space between us.

After a few seconds of awkward silence, Cardinal made a cute display of clicking her tongue. "Oh, come now, don't be coy."

Who, me or you?!

I felt her arms circle around my own back, and then a mild pressure on the fabric of my shirt. My forehead knocked her large hat off onto the table, and her curly brown hair brushed my cheek. There was a mild weight and warmth on my shoulder and chest.

"........."

I withstood the incredible pressure of the silence for as long as I could, then decided I would ask her what was happening. But Cardinal broke it first, her barely audible voice the only sound in the vast chamber.

"I see...So this," she said, exhaling deeply, "is what it means to be human..."

I gasped.

After two hundred years of thinking about every possibility and strategy, the final thing that Cardinal would want to know could be nothing other than the warmth of another human being.

No human being can survive alone; we are social creatures. To be human means to trade words with others, to join hands, to touch another's soul. And yet this girl had been isolated in this room with nothing but silent books for two hundred years.

At last, I felt I was beginning to understand the reality of the life Cardinal had lived to this point. My arms closed, pulling on her back to form a closer embrace.

"...You're warm..."

Something about the quality of her whisper was definitively different from her voice before. I could sense a small but undeniably warm drop of liquid slowly moving down my cheek.

"...At last...It's all been worth it...I didn't spend those two hundred years...for nothing..."

I felt another drop run down my cheek and disappear.

"Just learning of this warmth alone...has made it all worth it. I am satisfied..."

*   *   *

After a period of time (I couldn't be sure how long), I felt the sensation of moving air and found that my arms were empty again.

Cardinal was off her chair, picking up the toppled hat from the table. She patted it a few times and put it back on her head. When she turned back to me, pushing up her glasses, she was the businesslike sage once again.

"How long are you going to just stand there like a fool?"

"...Oh, come on...," I protested weakly, wondering if those tears had been a trick of the mind. I rested against the side of the table, folded my arms, and exhaled. Cardinal waited in silence until she brought up the big question, rather simply.

"So did you come to a conclusion? Will you take part in my plan or not?"

"..."

Sadly, I did not have the decisiveness to answer right on the spot.

In logical terms, picking ten names and pulling them out to the real world with Cardinal's help represented the best-case scenario. I could not have countered with a better idea.

But just because I couldn't think of one didn't mean it didn't exist. I wanted to believe there was a better option. So I looked Cardinal straight in the face and told her, "...All right. I'll take part in your plan. But..."

I spoke slowly, carefully. "But I'm not going to stop thinking about it. Even after we start fighting against the Integrity Knights and Administrator, I'm going to keep searching for a way—for a resolution that avoids the tragedy of the stress test and allows the world to stay at peace."

"You are quite the optimist. But I knew that about you already."

"It's just...I don't want you to disappear. And if ten is all I get to choose, you'll be one of them."

Her eyes widened briefly, then resumed their usual wry expression. Cardinal shook her head dramatically. "...And you are stupid, to boot. If I escape from the simulation, then who will wipe the world clean?"

"Like I said...I understand the concept, I'm just not going to stop struggling to find a better answer along the way."

She looked annoyed, then turned away from me. Her voice rode the little ripple of breeze from the whipping of her robe, bearing with it the vast loneliness of two centuries that a moment's embrace couldn't heal.

"Someday...you, too, will know the bitterness of resignation... Not from running out of strength and falling short...but being forced to admit that you will likely do so...Now let us return. Your partner will be finishing up that history book, I suspect. We ought to include Eugeo in the concrete planning stages."

She rapped her staff on the stone floor and headed down the way we came without a glance back at me.

2

As Cardinal predicted, Eugeo was just closing the cover of the heavy tome resting on his knees when we came across him sitting on the stairs. He looked dazed, still lost in that journey over centuries of history.

I strode up to him and said, "We're back. Sorry to have left you alone for so long."

For some reason, Eugeo shivered briefly, blinked hard, then looked toward me at last.

"Oh...Kirito. How long has it been...?"

"Huh? Uh..."

I looked around, but of course, there were no clocks in the room or even windows. Cardinal cleared her throat and answered, "Roughly two hours. The sun has risen by now. What did you think of the human world's long history?"

"Hmm...What can I say?" Eugeo replied, biting his lip and casting around for the right words. "...Is everything written in this book what actually happened? It just feels...like I'm reading a list of very convenient fairy tales. I mean, most of the entries are just, 'Such and such a problem arose at this place, the Integrity Knights resolved the matter, and after that point, such and such an entry was added to the Taboo Index'...That's all it is."

"But that is what historical record is. And the Axiom Church's style is to block each and every hole of the sieve until the water no longer passes through," Cardinal spat. Eugeo looked shocked. I couldn't blame him—I was sure he'd never heard someone openly criticize the Church that way, especially someone who appeared so young.

"Um...so, who are you...?"

"Oh, her name is Cardinal," I answered. "She's, uh...another, former pontifex. She got kicked out by the current pontifex, Administrator."

Eugeo made a strange sort of gulping sound deep in his throat and backed away.

"It's okay—you don't have to be afraid. She's going to help us fight against the Integrity Knights."

"H-help...?"

"That's right. She's got a mission to stop Administrator and restore her own rule over the world. So we're, uh...working for the same side," I said. It was extremely brief, and although I didn't lie to him, I wasn't about to explain that Cardinal's first act after she regained control would be to bring about the premature end of the Underworld. I'd have to talk to Eugeo about it eventually, but at this moment in time, I couldn't begin to guess how I'd broach the topic.

My partner, who was essentially the personified concept of *honesty* wearing clothes, stared at Cardinal without a shred of doubt in his eyes and grinned weakly. "I see...That's very good news, then. Well, if you were the old pontifex, doesn't that mean you can tell us if the Integrity Knight Alice Synthesis Thirty is the same person as Alice Zuberg from Rulid? And if so...is there a way to turn her back to her old self...?"

Cardinal looked downcast as she replied, "I'm sorry...but my sources of information from here are very limited. I only know what my modest number of familiars see and hear directly. My knowledge of the cathedral and the middle of Centoria is better, but the farther toward the frontier you go...I am aware of the birth of the Integrity Knight named Alice, but I have no means of knowing the details at this point..."

Eugeo looked crestfallen at first, then sucked in a sharp breath when he heard what came next.

"...However, I *can* teach you how to undo the Synthesis Ritual, the sacred art that creates an Integrity Knight."

Cardinal looked first at Eugeo, then at me, and intoned, "Simply remove the Piety Module that has been inserted into their souls."

"Pye...moju...?" Eugeo repeated, stumbling over the unfamiliar English ("sacred tongue") words.

I helpfully added, "*Module* is a sacred arts word that means, uh, *part*. Remember what we saw when we were fighting Eldrie in the rose garden? When he started acting weird..."

"Yeah...that purple crystal rod started coming out of his forehead..."

"Precisely," Cardinal said, using her staff to draw a line in midair and then bisecting it down the middle. "The Piety Module is designed to interrupt the connections between memories. Thus, it hides the future Integrity Knight's past and forces absolute fealty to the Axiom Church and pontifex. However, such a forceful and complex spell is not stable by nature. If those crucial base memories around the module are externally stimulated and activated, it can start to undo the effects of the spell, as you saw for yourselves."

"Meaning...to undo the sacred art, you have to force the knight to confront their old memories?" I asked excitedly, but Cardinal did not confirm.

"No, that would not be enough. There is another element that *must* be present."

"Wh-what is it?" Eugeo asked, leaning forward.

"It is what existed in the place where the module is inserted—in other words, the knight's most precious memories. Usually, this is their most deeply beloved person. Do you remember what you said to him to cause such a strong reaction?"

Eugeo already had it on the tip of his tongue before I could recall.

"Yes, it was his mother's name. That almost caused the crystal to fall out of his head."

"That would be it, then...Eldrie's memories of his mother

were removed, and the module was inserted to take their place. Administrator does not need *any* of the Integrity Knight's past, but memory is strongly tied to skill. If she removed all their memories, their ultimate strength as knights—sword skill, ultimate techniques, sacred arts—would be lost. So she merely impedes the flow of memories. I removed much of my own memory for the sake of prolonging my life, and much of the knowledge and ability I learned during that period was lost along with it..."

Cardinal then sighed and continued, "...To repeat, Administrator has taken the most precious memories of all the Integrity Knights. Unless you can regain those, even removing the Piety Module will not return the flow of memories to its prior state. And in the worst case, it might even damage the memories themselves."

"A piece of memory...But...then...what if the piece of memory that Administrator removes from the knights just gets destroyed?" I asked, hesitant to learn the answer.

Cardinal frowned as she thought it over, then said, "No...I do not think she would do that. Administrator is a cautious woman above all else—she would not discard something that could be used. But I am absolutely certain she would store them in her chamber at the top of Central Cathedral..."

The words *top of the cathedral* roused some part of my memory like a little jolt of electricity, but the sensation dissipated before I could pin it down. I tried to dispel the bad aftertaste by saying, "So we need those lost bits of memory to return the Integrity Knights to normal, but in order to get them, we have to break through the knights' guard and reach the top floor where Administrator is..."

"Do not presume that you can simply defeat the Integrity Knights without killing them," she said, glaring at me. "All I can do for you is give you equipment that is the equal of the knights'. The rest comes down to how hard you fight against them."

"Wait...You're not coming with us?" I said. I'd been counting on a helpful back-row mage with unlimited healing powers.

But Cardinal simply said, "If I leave the Great Library, Administrator will instantly detect my presence, and we will be forced to fight both her and the combined power of all her knights. But if you are confident that you can tackle ten Integrity Knights at once, we might try it. Well?"

She smirked at her suggestion, and Eugeo and I shook our heads in protest.

"On the other hand, Administrator still likely plans to take you two alive and make you into knights. If you leave alone, she will send a smaller number after you. Your only choice will be to defeat them in order and make your way up the cathedral."

"Hmm…"

True—when outnumbered, it was smarter to use ourselves as bait to split up the enemy as much as possible. But even succeeding in that sense, we were facing the most powerful fighters in the world. We'd had plenty of trouble against Eldrie alone. If we ever faced two at once, I had a feeling we'd be done for.

While I pondered, Eugeo took on a serious look and said, "All right. If we have to fight, we'll fight, and if we have to kill…then we have no choice. I was prepared for that from the moment we broke out of our cell. But…what if we have to face Alice? I can't fight against her—I'm here to get her back."

"Hmm. You are correct. I am aware of your quest, Eugeo. Very well, if you run across the Integrity Knight Alice, you may use these," Cardinal said, removing two very small daggers from the pocket of her black robe.

They were simply shaped, like crosses with the long end sharpened. The only decoration of any sort was a delicate chain running through a hole on the hilt of each. Cardinal gave us both one of the deep-copper stilettos. I reached out to grab the fragile handle between my fingertips and was stunned at its weight. It was less than eight inches long, but it felt as heavy as the official swords at the Swordcraft Academy.

"What's this…? Some kind of one-hit-kill superweapon?" I asked, dangling the dagger from the chain in front of my face to examine it.

"That dagger is only what it looks like; it has nearly no attacking power," Cardinal answered. "But anyone who is pierced by that blade will be instantly linked to me in the library via an unbreakable connection. In other words, any and all of my sacred arts are guaranteed to land on them. Those daggers are a part of me, you see. Eugeo, all you need to do is evade Alice's strikes and hit her with that knife, anywhere on her body. It will cause hardly any damage. I will instantly put Alice into a deep sleep, one that will last until you can regain her memories and prepare to undo the Synthesis."

"A deep...sleep...," Eugeo muttered, looking down at the dark-red blade in his hand with suspicion. He seemed to be grappling with the idea of harming Alice, even with a flimsy little paper knife.

I slapped him on the back and said, "Let's trust her, Eugeo. If we do have to fight against Alice and our only option is to knock her out, we'll all get pretty badly hurt, including her. Compared to that, a poke from this little thing is no worse than a greater swampfly bite."

"...Except they don't bite people," Eugeo corrected, seemingly back to his usual self. He turned to Cardinal and said, "All right. If we can't argue Alice down, I'll have to use this."

He gripped the dagger tight and nodded deeply to reassure himself. I let out a breath of relief and looked at my own cross-shaped knife.

"...Cardinal, you said this was a part of you, right? What's that supposed to mean?" I asked.

She shrugged. "Just because Administrator and I can generate any kind of object does not mean we fashion them from nothing."

"Huh...?"

"There is a finite amount of resources in the world. You know that from the way the Gigas Cedar prevented any fields from growing in its shadow. Along the same lines, if I want to generate an object of a certain priority level, I must sacrifice something of equal substance. When I battled against Administrator all those years ago, she summoned a sword, while I generated a staff—and at that exact moment, quite a few very valuable treasures vanished from her chamber, *heh-heh*."

She rapped the stone with the butt of her staff, looking rather pleased with herself. "But as you can see, the library is a closed-off space. I do not have any objects noteworthy enough to convert into a high-priority weapon. These countless books are, of course, very precious, but only due to their contents. I thought about using this staff, but I will need it to fight Administrator, which means that the only possible substitute to create these weapons is my own body. It is extremely valuable—I have the highest authority level possible in this world."

"Your..."

"Body...?"

Eugeo and I stared at her tiny, fragile form from head to toe. I could sense how rude I was being almost instantly and turned my eyes away, but not before confirming that she had all her limbs. I started to comment but stopped myself several times before I finally said, "...S-so, um...you cut off part of your body, converted it into an object...and then regrew the part...?"

"Fool! How would that be any kind of sacrifice? It is this."

She turned her head to the side and quickly ran her fingers through the short, bouncy curls of brown hair at the sides of her neck.

"Ohhhh...your hair..."

"The price for each dagger is a lock of hair that I was growing for two hundred years. If you had come sooner, I could have showed them off before I cut them," she teased, but I caught the hint of sadness in her eyes. Perhaps that part of Cardinal came from the young girl who made up her bodily foundation.

A moment later, she was the wizened sage once again. "For this reason, although they are small, the blades are sharp and tough enough to pierce the Integrity Knights' armor. And because they are still, in a sense, part of my body, they can link to me through the void that surrounds the library. I fashioned these weapons for direct use against Administrator. I will need you to plant the blade into her body without falling prey to her fierce attacks. The other is a backup weapon, but as long as you're successful the first time, you won't need it."

"Wow...talk about laying on the pressure..."

I glanced at the knife dangling from my right hand again and noticed that the shade of deep brown was the same as the hair visible underneath Cardinal's hat.

Despite the many confusing sacred words in the explanation, Eugeo seemed to accept the importance of the weapon. He stammered, "Umm...a-are you sure about this? You don't mind if I use one of these precious blades for Alice...?"

"I am fine with it. And in either case..."

She paused and looked right through me with those all-seeing eyes.

Yes, in either case, if I was going to bring ten souls back to the real world safely, including Eugeo and Alice, I would need Cardinal's help to undo Alice's brainwashing. It would probably be better to save this explanation until after we got Alice back to normal. If it was at the side of someone he truly cared about, Eugeo might actually agree to the escape plan. I *had* to make him agree.

I clenched the fine chain, realizing with no small frustration that I was already taking Cardinal's world-obliteration plan for granted. Perhaps the end of the Underworld really was inevitable at this point. But even if that was the case, I needed Cardinal to be one of those ten—even if I had to deceive her to do it.

I turned away to escape that omniscient gaze and opened my collar wider to slip the chain of the knife around my neck. Once Eugeo had done the same, I went back to something Cardinal had said earlier that bothered me.

"By the way...you said that there needed to be some kind of price to generate objects. So what did you use up to create all the food and drink when we first got here?"

Cardinal shrugged easily and grinned. "Don't let it bother you. Just two or three books of law that nobody will miss."

Eugeo the history buff made another strangled gulp, clutching the chain around his neck with both hands.

"Hmm? What, did you want more? You growing boys…"

She lifted her staff and made to wave it, but Eugeo's head and hands both waved frantically. "N-no, I'm full, I swear! I-I'd rather hear more of your story!!"

"You don't have to be shy," Cardinal muttered with a grin that was so cheeky, I could have sworn she was teasing him on purpose. She lowered the staff, cleared her throat, and continued, "We've gotten a bit out of order. As I explained earlier, those two knives are my secret weapon. Your top priority is to stab your targets with them: Alice for Eugeo and Administrator for Kirito. Do anything you can to raise your chances of success—ambush, playing dead, anything. If there is any way that I believe you outrank the Integrity Knights, it is your wiles…er, your practicality in a pinch."

Before Eugeo could lodge a righteous protest at that last comment, I said, "Completely agreed. If possible, I'd love to be able to utilize trickery all the way through…but sadly, they have the home advantage. We need to be outfitted for all-out combat. Earlier, you said you could give us equipment that was equal to that of the Integrity Knights, Cardinal. Does that mean you'll be giving us piles of Divine Object weapons and armor?"

Even in these desperate times, the old Aincrad instincts couldn't help but react to the scent of a legendary gear event. But in contrast to my eagerness, Cardinal put on yet another exasperated face and said, "Have you been listening to anything I say, fool? To generate a high-level object—"

"Right, right…you need to sacrifice an object of equal value… right…"

"Don't look like a child who just dropped his dessert on the floor! It is making me question why I asked you for help in the first place. For one thing, I believe you must realize that a weapon does not perfectly obey your commands from the moment you first touch it. No matter how powerful a blade I give you, it cannot hope to match the weapons the Integrity Knights have used as extensions of their very bodies for decades."

I recalled the way Eldrie's whip had moved through the air

with a mind of its own, like some silver snake, and had to concede the point. Even back in *SAO*, it was a kind of behavioral taboo to immediately put your new rare gear to real use without practicing with it first.

My disappointment was more than dropping a dessert on the ground—it was like missing out on an entire holiday cake. Her reaction a mix of annoyance and pity, Cardinal continued, "And besides, why would I need to give you powerful weapons when you already have excellent and familiar swords?"

"What?" Eugeo reacted instantly. "You're going to get back my Blue Rose Sword and Kirito's…black one?!"

"I see no other option. Those two swords are truly divine. One is the weapon of one of the four dragon knights, and the other is the essence of a demonic tree that absorbed vast resources for centuries. Even Administrator and I would find it difficult to instantly produce weapons of that scale. And you both have had plenty of practice with them."

"Oh…well, you could have mentioned that you can do that." I sulked, leaning back against the nearest shelf. I'd mostly given up on retrieving the swords that were confiscated when we got thrown into the dungeon. Getting them back was the best possible news.

"But…you can't actually teleport them directly here, can you?"

"No. I see you're finally figuring this all out," Cardinal said. She crossed her arms and looked troubled. "I suspect that your swords are being held in the armory on the third floor. The nearest back door will dump you out just thirty mels from there, but as you've now seen, any such door within the tower can be used only once. The insects that Administrator sends to look for me will swarm it at once, you see. So after you've left the door to get your swords in the armory, you will have to climb the tower on your own from there. Fortunately, the great stairs are right in front of the armory."

"Hmm, starting from floor three…and what floor is Administrator's chamber on?"

"Central Cathedral grows by the years, so I would guess…that it is close to a hundred floors by now…"

"A hund…"

My breath caught. True, the white tower was so tall that from any angle in Centoria, the top was always hidden from view… but I didn't think it would actually have more floors than some real-life skyscrapers. The thought of potentially having a fight on each and every floor was a bit much, so I whined, "Um, couldn't you start us at, like, the fiftieth floor instead…?"

"It's all in your perspective, Kirito," interjected Eugeo, who between the two of us was always the optimist by a factor of ten. "The longer it takes us to get there, the more spread out our enemies will be."

"…Uh, well, maybe that's true, but…"

I let my back slide farther down the side of the shelf until I was sitting on the ground. I mumbled, "Well…I did climb the outside stairs of the old Tokyo Tower once…"

"Huh?"

"Er, sorry, nothing. Anyway, I guess that decides our plan. First, we get the swords from the armory. Then we ascend the tower, defeating any Integrity Knights we encounter along the way. If we come across Alice, we put her to sleep with the knife and send her to the library. Once we reach the hundredth floor, we stab Administrator with the other knife and find Alice's memory fragment."

At last, I was feeling like we had a mission blueprint in place. Then Cardinal said, "I'm afraid there is one more thing you must do."

"Uh…wh-what's that?"

"Your swords are indeed powerful, but they will not be enough to beat the Integrity Knights. They have a means of amplifying the abilities of their weapons to many times their original value."

"Oh…you mean the Perfect Weapon Control thing…?" Eugeo asked hoarsely.

Cardinal explained, "Divine weapons take on significant qualities of the objects used as their foundation. Eldrie's Frostscale

Whip was once a two-headed white serpent that ruled the largest lake in the east, until Administrator took it alive and converted it into a weapon. But even as a dormant whip, it has the speed of a snake, the sharpness of its scales, and the accuracy of its aim. Perfect Control is the state of unleashing the weapon's memories and bringing about attacks that would normally be impossible."

"Great, so his whip turning into a snake wasn't some kind of illusion magic..." I groaned and rubbed the mark on my chest where Eldrie's whip had hit me, hoping that the white serpent didn't have some kind of slow-acting venom.

Cardinal continued, "All the Integrity Knights have Perfect Control over the weapons Administrator gave them—including mastery over the lengthy, speedy sacred arts commands to make use of them. You won't have much time to practice the chants, but at the very least, you must learn how to unlock Perfect Control of your swords, or our chances of victory are fleeting."

"But...my black sword wasn't even a living thing, it was just a huge tree...Is there even any memory to be unlocked there?"

"There is. Even that dagger I gave you harbors the memory—or nature—of my hair, so it can open a route to me when it lands, utilizing the same process as Perfect Control. Your sword, forged from the Gigas Cedar, and Eugeo's Blue Rose Sword, based on the eternal frost of the cave, are no exception to this pattern."

"Y-you mean...it's just...ice?" Eugeo gaped. I couldn't blame him; the only special property of ice that came to mind was that it was really, really cold. I puzzled over that one a bit and then decided if one of the two gods in this world said so, then it had to be true.

"Well...if you're going to teach us how to do it, then I'm assuming that this Perfect Control technique will work with our swords, too. I'd be happy to get some killer ultimate attack. What's it like?"

Once again, I was not expecting her response. "Don't be naive! I will describe how to unlock the technique, but what sort of attack style you make with it is entirely up to you."

"Uh…what?! How come?!"

"The core of Perfect Weapon Control is the Memory Release technique, but just chanting a sacred art alone is not enough. You must use your mind to imagine the unleashed form of your trusty weapon. In fact, it is this mental process of recall that is more crucial to your success than the Perfect Control technique itself. For it is the power of the imagination that forms the fundamental basis of the world—the ability to *incarnate* what you envision…"

I started losing track of the meaning of Cardinal's rapid-fire explanation partway through. In particular, I was uncertain whether the word *incarnate* was meant to be from the sacred or common tongue, but before I could ask her to elaborate, something prickled in the back of my memory.

It was…yeah, two and a half months ago. As I kneeled before the loose petals of the tattered zephilia flowers in the garden of Sword-craft Academy's primary dorm, someone—Cardinal's familiar, the little black spider Charlotte—whispered to me. She too had mentioned that all sacred arts were nothing but a tool to refine and collect the power of imagination.

I'd followed her suggestion and used my mind to envision the life energy of the four holy flowers in the nearby beds flowing into the severed plants. I didn't say a single word aloud, yet green light ran through the air, enveloped the buds…and brought the zephilias back to life.

That must have been the "process of recall," as Cardinal called it. In that sense, it would indeed seem to be impossible to express everything that phenomenon represented within the form of a sacred art command.

Cardinal gave me a serene, knowing nod and then turned to Eugeo, who still seemed to be struggling with this.

"Come with me. Let us take a break and then construct the arts."

We passed through the hallway of historical records, descended a number of staircases, and returned to the round room on the first floor of the library where we first appeared. On the table in the center sat the plates stacked with dumplings and sandwiches. Despite being at least two hours since they were served, the food was still steaming. In addition to healing the wounds of anyone who ate them, they apparently were also subjected to a spell that kept them from cooling off.

The sight inevitably rekindled my hunger, but knowing now that all this had originally been books from the library made it difficult to act. Cardinal noticed us grappling with our inner conflict and said indifferently, "If you will not eat more, I'll get rid of them. They'll only interfere with the mental process."

"W-wait, at least just put them somewhere that we can't see them. We'll take some to go when we leave," I pleaded. The girl shook her head, lifted her staff, and rapped the edge of the table. The huge plate sank directly into the surface, food and all.

Following that, three chairs pushed their way up out of the floor, which Cardinal motioned toward. I sat down in one and stared at the now empty tabletop.

Since the dumplings weren't going to be summoned again, I decided to focus my mind on the image of my absent sword—the temporarily named Black One—but found that, given the few times I'd actually used it, I could not imagine all the fine details.

Eugeo tried the same thing and had a similarly frustrating result. He wondered, "Cardinal...can we really do this? How am I supposed to imagine my weapon's unleashed form when it's not even here...?"

On the other side of the table, Cardinal said, to my surprise, "Its absence is better for the process. If you can see the weapon before your eyes, your imagination stops there. Your hands and eyes are not necessary to touch the hidden memory in the sword, guide it, and unleash it. You merely need the eye of the heart."

"The eye...of the heart," I repeated, recalling the moment when the zephilias came back to life. As a matter of fact, I hadn't touched either the holy flowers or the dying zephilias. I hadn't even focused on them. I just believed and envisioned—the life overflowing, gathering, moving.

Eugeo was nodding, as if he had found his own understanding. The black-robed sage grinned faintly and commanded, "Now, you must envision your swords resting on the tabletop. Do not stop until I say so."

"...All right."

"I'll give it a try."

We straightened up in our seats and focused on the empty table. Before, I'd tapped out after five seconds, but this time I kept staring; no need to rush. I started by emptying my mind.

The Black One. Thinking about it now, I realized that it was rather cruel of me to have referred to it by such a lazy temporary name all this time.

It took the craftsman Sadore an entire year to whittle the top branch of the Gigas Cedar down to the shape of a sword. He finished on March 7th. This was May 24th, so I hadn't had it for even three months yet. Excluding polishing and practice, the only times I'd pulled it from its sheath were in the battle against first-seat disciple Volo Levantein, and the true combat against this year's top student, Raios Antinous. That was it.

And in both cases, the black sword had helped me with stunning displays of power that seemed to come from nothing but its very own will—even though it was I who had cut down the Gigas Cedar from which it was made. Our history together was short, but when I gripped its handle and executed a sword skill with it, the sense of oneness and elation easily rivaled that of any other sword I'd used.

Perhaps the reason I hesitated to give this sword a proper name was due to its contrast with Eugeo's divine Blue Rose Sword.

White and black. Flower and tree. Two swords that were similar, but opposites in many ways.

Though I had no evidence for it, I'd been possessed by a certain foreboding ever since I'd left the village of Rulid two years ago. A vision of Blue Rose and black swords fated to cross one day.

My logical side told me it wasn't true. There was absolutely no reason that Eugeo and I, as the owners of the swords, would ever fight. But I got an intuitive sense that the same might not hold true for the swords themselves. For one thing, it was the Blue Rose Sword that actually cut down the Gigas Cedar...

Rather than emptying my mind, I was filling it with memories and reflections—but still I envisioned the black blade lying on the table. A simple, rounded pommel. The black leather wrapped around the grip. The bold curve of the guard. The blade, on the thick side, black and a little translucent, like crystal, and totally unlike any wood I'd ever seen. It collected the light inside and glinted along the edge and point, which were as fine and sharp as a razor...

The illusion of the sword, which had wavered uneasily in spots at first, began to grow firmer and more stable as my intruding thoughts gradually faded. Eventually it had a toughness, a weight, even a temperature. It exuded a powerful sense of presence on the table.

As I gazed into the shining flat of the blade, I heard a voice from somewhere say, "Deeper. You must dive deeper, until you can touch the memory hidden in the sword, its true essence."

The black of the sword expanded without a sound. It covered the table, the floor, the bookshelves and lamps, and then the world. Only the sword and I existed in this infinite, lightless space. It rose up and came to a halt in the air, handle down and point up. My form rippled and melted, and I felt my mind getting sucked into the sword.

The next thing I knew, I was a cedar tree rooted in cold ground.

It was a deep forest, and yet there wasn't a single tree growing around me. I stood alone in a rounded clearing. I tried to call out to the moss and narrow vines crawling along the ground at my feet, but there was no answer.

...Solitude.

I was racked with desolate loneliness. With each breeze, I stretched my branches desperately, hoping to rustle against the others, but I came up short every time.

Maybe I could reach them if I stretched farther. So I sucked in ground energy through my roots and light energy through my leaves. My trunk thickened, and my branches extended. My needlelike leaves stretched, grasping toward the shining green leaves of the closest oak.

Alas! Just before I could finally make contact, the oak leaves turned brown, wilted, and fell all at once. The moisture drained out of the branches and even the trunk; it weakened and died, then toppled over from the base. And it wasn't just the oak. All the trees at the rim of the rounded clearing were dying and crumbling. Soon their remains, too, were covered by the carpet of moss.

I lamented my solitude in the now larger clearing, then sucked strength from the ground and sun again. My trunk swelled, creaking, and my branches expanded. This time I reached for the next closest tree, a laurel.

Once again, its leaves wilted before I could touch them, the dead trunk rotted, and it toppled. So did the tree next to it. And the one after. More and more trees fell, and the empty space grew larger.

Because I was sucking up power to stretch my branches, the other trees were dying. But even understanding this, I did not stop trying to touch them. How many times did I repeat the same thing? Eventually, I was dozens of times the size of the other trees, and the clearing itself was dozens of times its original span. The same could be said of my loneliness.

No matter how hard I reached, the day would never come when my pointed needles made contact with the leaves of another tree. But by the time I realized this, it was too late to turn back. My leaves and branches gobbled up incredible amounts of sun, regardless of my wishes, and the vast lattice of my roots devoured the power of the earth. The cold empty space grew by the day as the trees fell over dead, one after another after another...

"That is enough," said a sudden voice, freeing me from the cedar.

I blinked once, and instantly I was back in the Great Library, surrounded by an endless array of bookshelves lit by orange lamplight, resting on polished stone floor. Before me was a round table, upon which sat two swords. My Black One and Eugeo's

Blue Rose Sword. They both looked totally real, but this could not be true. Both of them were gone, confiscated when we were thrown into the cells.

As I sat gazing emptily at the white and black swords, a small hand reached out from the other side of the table and grabbed the handle of the black sword first. It wavered, then vanished in silence. Next, she brushed the Blue Rose Sword. Again, it blinked away as though sucked up into her palm.

"......Aye. I've received the memories of the swords that you have brought forth," Cardinal said with satisfaction. I looked into the eyes of the black-robed girl across the table—and only then did I realize I had fallen into a kind of trance. Next to me, Eugeo's green eyes wandered dully, then he suddenly jolted and blinked.

"...Huh...? I was just...on the highest peak...of the End Mountains," he murmured.

I couldn't help but smirk. "You were all the way up there, man?"

"Yeah. It was incredibly cold and extremely lonely..."

"Do not relax yet," scolded Cardinal. I sat upright, realizing we'd been getting into chitchat mode. The little sage had her eyes closed. Her brows drew together slightly in concentration, and then she nodded.

"Aha...I believe that simplifying the command is preferable to tweaking the technique itself. I shall start with your sword, Kirito."

She tapped the table with her left hand, silently producing a sheet of blank parchment. She then brushed the sheet with her other hand, sliding from top to bottom.

That simple action produced at least ten lines of command text. She spun the sheet around and slid it over to me, then repeated the process for Eugeo. The two of us shared a look and then glanced down to examine our sheets.

The text, written in blue-black ink, was entirely in the sacred script (meaning the alphabet), with no commands in the common tongue (Japanese). In orthodox sacred arts format, the list was numbered down the left, with each entry's command to the right. Starting from *System Call* at the top and ending with *Enhance Armament* on line ten, there were at least twenty-five command words in the list.

That was shorter than the Perfect Control that Eldrie used on his Frostscale Whip, to be sure, but it was still a major task to memorize it all.

"Ummm…I don't suppose I could keep this as a cheat sheet…"

"Of course not. Not even a fresh-faced new student at the academy would be allowed to peek at the text when demonstrating their practical skill," Cardinal chided. "For one thing, if you removed any object connected to this library and it fell into enemy hands, that might lead to the unraveling of my spatial isolation."

"B-but…those knives…"

"Those are linked to me personally—that's different. Now get to memorizing and stop whining. Eugeo's already working on his."

My head whipped around, and to my shock, goody-two-shoes Eugeo was already gazing intently at the list, his lips moving soundlessly. I gave up and looked back at my own list, just as Cardinal added a cruel condition to the exercise.

"You have thirty minutes to memorize this list."

"Aw, come on…," I protested. "What is this, an exam? At least give us more time to—"

"*Fool!*" she thundered. "Listen to me: Your swords were confiscated when you were locked up at eleven o'clock the previous morning. Your ownership of the items will reset after twenty-four hours, which means you will no longer be able to utilize this Perfect Weapon Control at all!"

"Oh…r-right. And what time is it now…?"

"Well after seven o'clock. Even allowed a full two hours to recover the weapons, you have very little time left."

"……Um, okay," I admitted, giving the command list my undivided attention this time.

Fortunately for me, the sacred arts of the Underworld, unlike magic spells in *ALfheim Online*, used familiar English terminology.

The format was similar to programming language, so my memorization was aided by understanding the words, not just the sounds.

The command list Cardinal wrote out was split into three major processes: (1) Accessing the object's deep data (the sword's memory) stored in the memory module; (2) selecting and molding the necessary portions alone; and (3) applying them to the current form of the sword to expand attack power. The methodology was similar to the "image buffer overwriting" experiment I tried out on the zephilia flowers back at the dorm, but none of the terms used were from the academy's textbooks, meaning that only Cardinal would be able to come up with this combination, due to her knowledge of the entire command list.

Even as I committed the ten commands to memory, a small part of my mind wandered.

The Rath scientists who had created the Underworld called the data format that recorded all the objects in this world *mnemonic visuals*. Over two years (of my personal subjective time) ago, at Agil's bar in Okachimachi in the real world, I had explained the broad concept to Asuna and Sinon. Through observation and experimentation, I had learned some things during my time here since.

The Underworld, unlike traditional VRMMOs, was not made of polygonal models. A processor called the Main Visualizer read and buffered the sum experiences of all those who connected to—or lived in—the world, from rocks and trees to dogs and cats, tools, buildings, and so on. When needed, it would extract the necessary information to display to the diver. The reason I was able to grow the zephilia flowers that shouldn't have grown in the northern empire was that I'd temporarily overwritten the average buffer data ("It doesn't grow here") with the mental image that said it *could* grow.

Furthermore: All objects in this world were saved as memories.

So wouldn't the reverse be true as well? Could memories be turned into objects? I had seen something before that I couldn't explain in any other way.

Two years and two months ago, when I first awoke in the forest south of Rulid, I wandered until I reached the banks of the Rul River. When I did, I was faced with an incredibly vivid image: that of a flaxen-haired boy and a blond girl walking against the backdrop of the setting sun—and a boy with short black hair, too.

The image had vanished in a matter of seconds, but it was no trick of the eyes. Even now, if I closed my lids, I could see the burning red sunset, the light glinting off the girl's waving hair, and the sounds of the kids treading through the grass. I had called the trio of children from my own memory. Obviously, one boy was Eugeo. The girl had to be Alice. And the black-haired boy...

"That's thirty minutes. How do you feel?" Cardinal said, cutting off the line of thought running through the back of my mind.

I flipped over the sheet of parchment and envisioned the command from the start. For not giving it my undivided concentration, I was relieved to find that I could recall every last word. "I've got it probably perfect."

"That was somewhat of an oxymoron. How about you, Eugeo?"

"Uh...um, I think I've got it probably per...probably fine."

"Very good," Cardinal said, stifling a smirk. "Just so you know, while Perfect Control is a powerful technique, it must not be used at every single opportunity. Its use consumes a considerable amount of the sword's life. On the other hand, it doesn't do to save it up if you are about to fall. Gauge the moment; use it wisely. Afterward, you must return it to its sheath and allow the life to recover."

"That sounds...tough...," I grumbled, then I flipped the parchment over again. I ran my eyes over the full command one more time for good measure and noticed something. "Huh? Wait a sec...The last phrase of this command is *Enhance Armament*, right?"

"Is there something wrong with that?"

"N-no, that's not what I mean. When we fought Eldrie, the Perfect Weapon Control technique he used had something else after that. It was, like, um...R...Rele...," I mumbled.

Eugeo stepped in to finish. "Release Recollection, I think. It was after he said *that* that his whip turned into a real snake. Boy, that really startled me."

"Yeah, exactly. Don't we need something like that, too, Cardinal?"

"Hrm," the black-robed sage grumbled, looking annoyed. "Listen, there are two stages to Perfect Weapon Control: Enhancing and Release. Enhancing recalls specific portions of the weapon's memory to unlock more attack power. And Release, as the name would suggest, unlocks and recalls *all* of the weapon's memory to unleash its wildest power."

"Wildest power, huh…I guess that explains it. With Eldrie's whip, he strengthened it to increase its range and split it into multiple parts, and then he released it so that it turned into a snake and attacked of its own will…"

Cardinal blinked in affirmation and said, "Precisely so. But I must be clear up front that this is still beyond your means."

"Wh-why?" asked Eugeo, clearly surprised.

The sage intoned, "It is the weapon's wildest power, as I said. The strength created by Release Recollection is beyond the ability of a new wielder to control, especially for a divine-level weapon. It will harm you as much as the enemy—perhaps even be fatal to you."

"P-point taken," said my partner, ever the obedient schoolboy. I had no choice but to accept her terms, too. But Cardinal could sense I was unconvinced, so she added, "The time will come when you can make use of Release…perhaps. The sword will teach you everything. But that assumes you can get it back first."

"Yeah, yeah," I muttered.

Cardinal rolled her eyes and tapped the base of her staff against the floor. The two parchments rolled themselves up on their own and even seemed to shrink—only to be replaced by long, narrow baked goods.

"You must be hungry after all that thinking. Eat up."

"Huh…? Are these magic treats that'll help us remember the commands or something…?"

"Of course not."

"Oh. Right."

Eugeo and I shared a look, then we picked up the sweets. At first, I thought they were the simple flour pastries with sugar sprinkled on top like the kind you could buy from the market in Centoria, but in fact, they were a much more real-world kind of delicacy: flaky piecrust coated with white chocolate. The combination of crispy texture and rich sweetness was so reminiscent of the real world that it nearly brought tears to my eyes.

We raced to see who would finish first, and once I was done, I looked up with a sigh of satisfaction into Cardinal's gentle, understanding eyes.

The young sage nodded slowly and said, "Now...it is time for good-byes."

There was such a weight to that brief statement, I couldn't help but deny it. "But once we complete our goals, you'll be able to come out safely, right? *Good-bye* seems a little dramatic..."

"That is correct. Assuming all goes well, of course..."

"..."

True, if we lost to the Integrity Knights at any point on our mission to reach the top of the cathedral, Cardinal would be forced to undergo another long, long wait. In fact, the stress test would probably arrive before she found another assistant, plunging the world into blood and flame.

But despite the looming, tragic catastrophe waiting in the wings, Cardinal's smile was pure and gentle. I felt an odd sensation clutch at my chest, and I bit my lip. She nodded almost imperceptibly and spun around.

"Come. It is time. Follow me...and I will send you through the door closest to the third-floor armory."

The walk from the first-floor library hall back to the entrance room with its countless back doors was disappointingly short.

Under his breath, Eugeo silently mouthed the commands for his Perfect Weapon Control technique, while my eyes never left the small figure of Cardinal leading the way.

I wanted to talk more. I wanted to know more about what she had thought and felt during those two hundred years in solitude. The sensation that I *needed* to know these things clawed its way up to my throat, but her pace was so quick and resolute that it brooked no discussion.

Once we were in the familiar chamber with countless hallways leading off the three other walls, Cardinal beckoned us toward one on the right side. Only after walking down the thirty-foot hallway to the simple door waiting at the end did she finally stop and turn back to us.

The smile on her pink lips was as gentle as ever. There was even a hint of a certain satisfaction there.

In a crisp, clear tone, she said, "Eugeo...and Kirito. The fate of the world now rests on you two. Whether it is plunged into hellfire...or sinks into oblivion. Or," she added, staring right at me, "if you find a third way. I have told you all that I can tell and given you all that I can give. As for the rest, simply follow in your beliefs."

"...Thank you, Cardinal," Eugeo said, his voice brimming with determination. "I know I'll reach the top of Central Cathedral... and bring Alice back."

I felt like I should say something, too, but no words came. Instead, I simply bowed my head in respect.

Cardinal nodded resolutely, her smile now gone, and she grabbed the knob.

"Now...go!"

She turned it and, in the next moment, flung the door wide open. Eugeo and I pushed against the sudden rush of cold, dry air and leaped through.

After five or six steps, I heard a small noise behind me and looked over my shoulder to see nothing but cold, smooth marble wall. There wasn't a single trace of the door to the Great Library.

CHAPTER EIGHT

CENTRAL CATHEDRAL, MAY 380 HE

1

How very, very far we've come...

The ceiling was high enough that he had to crane his neck to see. Pillars of marble stood all around, and the floor was a fine mosaic of different kinds of stones fitted together.

Eugeo could scarcely breathe upon his first glimpse of the grand interior of the Axiom Church's Central Cathedral. Until two years ago, his entire life, as far as he knew it, was to be vainly swinging an ax into a tree that would never fall down. His only sentiment would be to reflect on the memories of his long-lost golden-haired friend as he led a lonely life without marriage or children, dwelling deep in the forest until the day he grew old and handed the ax to a new generation and passed away with no one to tell his tale.

It was the sudden arrival one day of a black-haired young man that had broken Eugeo's tiny, suffocating world by force. Using methods the previous carvers could never have imagined, he had cut down the absolute barrier blocking the way to the big city and confronted Eugeo with a major decision: stay here in his tiny home, nursing his memories of Alice, or set out on a massive journey to get her back?

It would be a lie to claim that he had never given it a second thought. When Chief Gasfut asked him what he wanted his next Calling to be on the night of the village festival, he had first considered his family.

Up to that point, Eugeo had given his family his entire salary as the Gigas Cedar carver. They were traditionally a barley-farming family, but their fields were small, and the recent run of poor harvests had left them little income. Eugeo's steady monthly wages were a minor bedrock that he knew his parents and brothers relied upon, even if no one wanted to admit it.

Once the Gigas Cedar was felled, that salary was gone, naturally. But if he chose to be a farmer, like his father, they would receive preferential choice of the large, sunny stretches ready to be tilled to the south. Standing at the pulpit amid the excited villagers, Eugeo looked into the hopeful and anxious faces of his family members.

His hesitation had lasted only an instant. On one end of the scale was a reunion with his childhood friend, and on the other was the livelihood of his family. The scale tilted, and Eugeo announced that he would leave the village and be a swordsman.

Even as a swordsman, he could choose to stay in Rulid and be one of the men-at-arms, ensuring he'd still have a salary. But leaving the village meant leaving his family. The money that Eugeo made and the possibility of new, fertile fields would all go up in smoke. He hastily left the day after the festival because he couldn't stand seeing the suppressed disappointment and unhappiness in the faces of his parents and brothers.

There had been more opportunities to choose a life that supported his family after he and Kirito left Rulid. They competed in the swordfighting tournament in Zakkaria and won the right to join the garrison there. After hard training, they were given a recommendation to North Centoria Imperial Swordcraft Academy—but the commander also offered to keep them around, with the promise of promotions and maybe even a future place as the garrison commander. If he'd accepted that steady salary in Zakkaria and had sent some of it back to Rulid on the regular trading caravan, it could have made things so much easier for his family.

And yet, Eugeo had turned down the commander's offer and accepted the letter of recommendation instead.

Along the way to Centoria, and even after joining the academy, a part of Eugeo's mind had been busy making excuses. He'd be named school representative, win the Four-Empire Unification Tournament, and receive the prestigious rank of Integrity Knight—and *then* his parents would have riches and comfort beyond their imagination. When he made his triumphant return with Alice, riding a dragon and outfitted in silver armor, his parents would be prouder of their youngest son than anyone could ever be.

But two nights ago, when he had drawn his blade against Raios Antinous and Humbert Zizek, Eugeo had betrayed his family for the third time. He gave up on the very real possibility of noble rank in his future…and chose to violate the Taboo Index, sacrificing his common status in the process.

Even as overwhelming rage drove his actions, a part of Eugeo had understood that if he attacked, he would lose everything. And yet, still he made the choice to go ahead. He could say it was to uphold his personal sense of justice and save Tiese and Ronie from being raped, but that wasn't all of it. He wanted to unleash the raging thirst to kill, to erase all traces of Raios and Humbert from the world. There was a pit of black desire in his heart.

How very, very far he had come…

From one of twelve elite, prestigious students at the academy to a traitor against the Axiom Church—and now there he was, stepping on the most hallowed ground in the entire world.

After escaping from the archer knight and winding up in a vast, enigmatic library, the little girl who claimed to be the previous pontifex of the Church showed him books full of the world's history, which he practically devoured. He had a pressing question to answer: How many people, in the long arc of history, had ever defied the Church, fought the Integrity Knights, achieved their desires, and safely escaped?

Sadly, he didn't find a single anecdote of such a thing in the historical record. The glory of the Church illuminated the world, and all peoples bowed before the might of the Integrity Knights. These things easily solved even the gravest of troubles—imperial border squabbles, for example. No matter how far he dug into the thick history tomes, he found no instances of anyone attacking the Church and fighting the knights.

That means that in 380 years of history, ever since Stacia created the world, I am the most sinful person who has ever lived.

He felt a freezing chill assault him as he closed the book. If Kirito hadn't returned at that very moment, he might have fallen to the ground and curled up into a ball.

Even as the mysterious little former pontifex explained the ways of the world to them, Eugeo couldn't help but grapple with himself. He'd abandoned his family, attacked another person, and chosen to fight the Church. He could never go back to his old life. The only way out was forward—bloodied hands, soiled soul, and all. There was just one goal ahead of him.

He had to retrieve the heart fragment stolen by the pontifex, turn Alice Synthesis Thirty back into Alice Zuberg, and take her home to Rulid Village.

But his hope for actually living with her was probably gone by now. There was no place he could live after his many sins anymore, except for the horrifying Dark Territory beyond the End Mountains. But even that was a price worth paying if it meant Alice could go back home and live in happiness again.

Eugeo watched Kirito walk before him, turning over this secret determination in his head. *If I said I was going to the Dark Territory, would you come with me...?*

He stopped himself before he could imagine his partner's answer. The black-haired boy was the only person in the entire world standing in this position with him. The idea that they might travel separate paths in the not-too-distant future was too frightening to ponder.

As Cardinal had warned, the hallway from the doorway was surprisingly short. He barely had time to get lost in his thoughts before they arrived at a spacious rectangular room.

In the center of the right-hand wall was a surprisingly large staircase leading upward. The ceiling was about eight mels above, so there were a good twenty steps before the stairs stopped at a landing. On the left-hand wall was a set of large double doors surrounded by sculptures of winged beasts.

Kirito flung out his hand and pressed against the wall, so Eugeo followed his lead and backed against a nearby pillar. They held their breath and listened intently for any presence in the dim chamber.

If the former pontifex was correct, those doors on the left would lead to the armory. For being so important, however, the chamber was silent and appeared empty. Even the light of Solus coming down from the stairs on the right seemed chilly and gray.

"...Looks like there's no one here...," he whispered to Kirito, who seemed a bit surprised.

"It's an armory, so you'd figure there would at least be a soldier or two on guard...but I guess nobody's going to sneak into the Axiom Church to steal weapons, anyway..."

"Still, they know *we're* here, right? They don't seem too concerned."

"They probably aren't. They figure they don't need to bother searching around for us. So the next time we run across an Integrity Knight, it'll either be a whole bunch of them or a really tough individual. Let's make the most of our leeway, then," Kirito said, finishing with a snort. He darted out from the shadow of the wall, and Eugeo followed him across the empty room.

The doors of the armory, carved with reliefs of the goddesses Solus and Terraria, were so imposing and stately that even without a keyhole, it almost seemed to suggest that they would not open to anyone who wasn't pure of faith. Kirito put an ear to one of the doors and yanked on the handles. They opened with almost disappointing ease—there wasn't even the squeak of a hinge.

The dark space beyond the fifty-cen opening exuded the chill of centuries of silence. Eugeo shivered, then had to hurry to squeeze through after Kirito entered without a care. The doors swung heavily shut behind them, leaving them in perfect darkness.

"System Call..."

Their voices spoke in perfect unison, and in spite of the dead-serious situation, Eugeo couldn't help but smile. The rest of the command was *Generate Luminous Element*, which reminded Eugeo of the time they'd gone to find Selka in the Northern Cave two years ago. At the time, even the simplest of beginning sacred arts was unbelievably hard to execute, and they could only weakly light the end of a stick.

A source of pure white light appeared above his palm, driving away the thick darkness and Eugeo's wistful recollection along with it.

"Whoa...," Kirito murmured. Eugeo swallowed.

What incredible size. The word *armory* had called to mind a space like the supply closet at the academy, but nothing could be further from the truth here. It was at least as big as the great training hall where Kirito had sparred with Volo Levantein.

The light element danced upward from Eugeo's palm, reflecting off all the polished stone walls—and more importantly, off shining metal of every variety and color.

The floor was packed with wooden stands for full sets of armor. Black armor, white armor, bronze, silver, gold—a blinding array of shades, as well as shapes, from light chain and boiled leather to seamless slabs of heavy plate. There had to be at least five hundred sets in the room.

And hanging all over the high walls was an assortment of what appeared to be every conceivable weapon. Even with swords alone, there were long and short ones, thick and slender, straight and curved. There were single- and double-bladed axes, spears, lances, war hammers, whips, bludgeons, and bows—every possible variation of weaponry in uncountable numbers, stretching from floor to ceiling. Eugeo's mouth dropped open and hung there.

"...If Sortiliena ever saw this place, she might just pass out," Kirito finally whispered, breaking the silence after many seconds.

"Yeah...I think Golgorosso would have leaped onto that greatsword there and never let go," Eugeo muttered, letting out his breath at last. He looked around the room again and shook his head a few times.

"I don't get it…Is the Church going to form its own army or something? You'd think the Integrity Knights were enough…"

"Hmm…To fight the forces of darkness? No, not quite," Kirito murmured, looking pensive. Then he turned to his friend. "It's the opposite. They're not creating an army…they've collected all these weapons to keep one from being created. I bet all these things are Divine Objects, or the next best thing to them. Administrator must have been worried about any other group getting these powerful weapons, so she gathered them all here to keep that strength out of the hands of others…"

"Huh…? What does that mean? No group would ever fight back against the Axiom Church, even if they did have powerful weapons."

"Maybe it means that the one with the least faith in the Church's power is the pontifex herself," Kirito said drily. Eugeo didn't understand that at first, and his partner patted him on the back before he could figure it out. "C'mon, we don't have time. Let's find our swords."

"Uh…y-yeah. It'll be hard to pick them out of here, though…"

The Blue Rose Sword and the Black One were in white and black leather scabbards with little ornamentation, and there were a number of similar-looking blades along the walls.

"…We probably used up too many spatial resources with that light element to use darkness search arts again," Eugeo lamented, wishing that they'd only cast *one* light instead of two.

Then Kirito simply said, "Oh! Found 'em." He pointed back, just to the left of the doorway they'd just walked through.

"Whoa…there they are."

Indeed, there was a white and black pair of swords in that direction, undeniably the ones belonging to them. Eugeo gazed at his partner in disbelief. "Kirito, how did you know without using sacred arts…?"

"I figured that if they were the last ones brought here, they'd be closest to the door." Kirito shrugged. Normally he'd have a proud, childish smirk on his face in this kind of situation, but now he was staring pensively at his sword. Then he exhaled, relaxed, and walked over to grab the black leather scabbard.

He paused for the briefest of moments, then lifted it off the display holder. He grabbed the Blue Rose Sword with his other hand and tossed it over. Eugeo hastily reached out to catch it and felt a familiar weight on his wrists.

He'd been separated from his blade for less than two days, but even he was surprised at the sudden surge of sentiment and relief as he clutched the sheath in both hands.

Ever since they felled the Gigas Cedar in his hometown, the Blue Rose Sword had been at his side. It had helped him through several great challenges, from the tournament in Zakkaria to the entrance duel at Swordcraft Academy, and even when he broke the Taboo Index to cut off Humbert's arm.

If the Axiom Church had been stockpiling powerful weapons for years and years, then it was nothing short of miraculous good luck that the Blue Rose Sword had been sleeping undisturbed in that cave for centuries. It was fate—proof that their route to taking Alice back was correct...

"Don't just stand there drinking it in; strap it on already," Kirito chided him. Eugeo came back to his senses and saw that his partner had already fastened his sheath to his sword belt. He smiled awkwardly and did the same, then patted the hilt with satisfaction. The expensive-looking sets of armor had nameplates displayed nearby with impressive names like Armor of a Thousand Thunderbolts and Quake Mountain Plate.

"...What do you think, Kirito? There are so many, I'm sure we can find some armor that fits us."

"No, we've never worn armor before. It's better not to try something you're not used to. Let's just take some clothes from over there," he replied, pointing to the end of the line of armor, where a variety of colorful outfits waited. Eugeo looked down at his own school uniform, which was dirty and torn from two days' use, the battle against Eldrie, and the frantic escape afterward.

"You're right. Pretty soon these will be more tatters than clothes."

The two light elements overhead were starting to dim. Eugeo abandoned his hope for armor and pored through the expensive-looking fabrics until he found shirts and pants that seemed the right size for them. They turned their backs for privacy and got to changing.

Eugeo ran his arms through the ultramarine shirt, which was very similar in tone to his school uniform, and marveled at the smoothness of its texture. He turned around and found that Kirito was reacting in a similar way, running his hands over the black fabric.

"...I bet these clothes have some kind of special origin, too. Let's hope they can help stop the Integrity Knights' attacks."

"Don't get your hopes up too high." Eugeo chuckled, then got serious. "So...shall we go?"

"Yeah...let's do it."

They returned to the entrance. Everything so far had been going so easily, it almost felt wrong—but that wouldn't last long. They shared a moment of knowing determination—ready for anything that might come—as they each took a door handle, Eugeo on the right and Kirito on the left.

They pulled gently, just barely opening it a crack, when—

Thak-thak-thak! A number of metal arrows thudded into the outer surface of the thick doors.

"Whoa!"

"What the—?"

The force of the impact knocked the doors farther inward, sending both Eugeo and Kirito tumbling to the floor.

Standing on the landing at the top of the great staircase on the other side of that rectangular entrance hall was a knight wearing familiar red armor, notching fresh arrows—four at once, in fact—to a longbow as tall as he was. It was the Integrity Knight who had chased them around the rose garden on the dragon.

The range between both was about thirty mels. It was way too far for a sword to reach but close enough for a master archer to strike with perfect accuracy. They wouldn't have time to pull

their swords free, much less recover from their fall and scramble to safety behind the walls.

This is why I wanted the armor! We could have had shields! Eugeo protested to no one but himself, right as the knight began to draw back the string.

Forget about escaping harm. They had to focus on avoiding a fatal blow, or at least a debilitating one.

Eugeo stared hard at the line of four arrows. The dull silver tips seemed trained not on their hearts but their legs. As Cardinal suggested, the knights appeared to be ordered to take them alive, not dead. But from their perspective, the two things might as well have been the same.

The Integrity Knight's bowstring creaked.

A moment of silence, in which everything short of time itself stopped.

Then Kirito's voice ripped through it: "Burst Element!"

It was so quick that Eugeo didn't actually pick up what his partner said at the time. It only clicked for him once he saw the result.

Instantly, his entire vision went white. Powerful light, like the descent of Solus itself, filled the room. It was a simple spell that released light, one of the elements that made up the building blocks of elemental sacred arts, but Kirito had never actually made the chant to produce the element in the first place. So where did it...?

Oh. It had been there all along—the light elements they created to illuminate the armory many minutes ago. Ever since, they had been floating around, waiting for the command input that would utilize them. Kirito simply gave that command to the elements overhead, producing a sudden burst of light.

Between this and the way he threw the shattered piece of glass in the fight against Eldrie, he's always had a knack for making use of whatever's nearby, Eugeo thought. He willed strength into his legs and leaped to the right.

Half a second later, he heard the unpleasant sound of metal arrows gouging stone coming from the spot where he'd just been.

He was going to continue moving to the safety of the wall, but then he heard Kirito shout, "Forward!"

Instantly, he understood the intention and launched himself: not diagonal, but *directly* forward.

The light elements had burst behind their heads, meaning that they hadn't seen the actual source of light directly, but the Integrity Knight most certainly had. They would have a few seconds with an opponent who couldn't see.

Light elements were weak in attack power compared to heat or freezing elements, and in fact were more often used in healing magic, but causing a weapon to flash could have blinding or menacing effects. The class at the academy claimed that theoretically, one should counteract the use of light elements in battle with their anti-element, dark.

As the pinnacle of sword and sacred arts ability, an Integrity Knight would naturally be aware of this basic knowledge, so they couldn't count on the light-based blindness trick to work twice. This was their first and only chance to close the distance on the ranged fighter.

Over and over, Kirito had told Eugeo that quick adaptation and smart action formed the core of the Aincrad style. It was the opposite way of thinking from the High-Norkia style, which emphasized grace and stylistic movement. And in order to keep your head about you and apply the teachings of the Aincrad style, it was essential to keep its secret motto in mind: "Stay cool."

Eugeo pelted after his partner as best he could, drawing the Blue Rose Sword from his left side as he went. Immediately afterward, the light element was spent, and proper color returned to the world. They were out of the armory and into the antechamber. Twenty steps up the staircase on the other side of the room, they saw the Integrity Knight still standing in place.

As expected, he continued to appear partially blinded. He had his hand up to the visor of his dark-red helm, his upper half swaying.

Fortunately for them, unlike Eldrie, this knight did not have a sword at his side. Going into battle indoors with only a longbow was a bold, confident move. He seemed to believe that he could still hit their legs with perfect accuracy as they approached.

Even with his mind cold and clear, Eugeo couldn't deny that there was a little flicker of anger in his head.

Sir Knight, you're just like Raios—proud, haughty, and perfectly assured of your own righteousness. You believe it makes you impervious. But that will be your undoing. I'm going to make sure you realize that!!

He charged up the great staircase, propelled by this rather unfamiliar emotion. One step, two steps, and on the third—

The knight removed his hand from his helmet visor and swung it behind his back, then pulled out more metal bolts from his quiver. All of them at once, in fact.

When he brought it back around, there were at least thirty arrows clutched in his hand. Before Eugeo could even wonder what he was going to do with that many, the knight arrayed the entire bundle along the length of the horizontal bowstring.

"Wha...?!"

Eugeo gasped and halted, right at the third step of the stairs. It couldn't be possible to shoot thirty arrows from a single bowstring at once and have them fly accurately.

He heard the sound of creaking metal. A shiver ran down his spine when he realized it was the sound of the arrows steadily giving way under an immense grip. Kirito had stopped to the right of him, unsure of the knight's true intention. Was it a desperate bluff, or was he really going to—?

The longbow yanked back all at once, with a louder creaking sound than before.

"Back and to the left!" Kirito bellowed.

The air *twang*ed and then snapped as the string finally gave out. But the thirty arrows flew in a radial pattern, a fatal silver sheet raining down on their heads from above.

Eugeo pushed so hard he thought his leg would break, hurtling himself to the left and holding his sword along the length of his body like a shield.

If the knight's vision had been perfect, they would have easily been pumped full of holes. One arrow struck the Blue Rose Sword and clanged away. Another caught the right hem of Eugeo's trousers, another ripped the skin of his left flank, and yet another grazed his left cheek, taking a few hairs with it.

Once his shoulder slammed onto the floor, Eugeo looked down, gritting his teeth in preparation for what he would see. After he realized he wasn't hurt too badly, he glanced over at Kirito, who had gone in the opposite direction.

"Kirito! You okay?" he shouted. His black-haired partner looked a little shaken as he replied, "Y-yeah, somehow. I think it actually went between my toes."

Eugeo saw that there was an arrow in the toe of Kirito's left shoe, the tip poking through the sole. He exhaled, thankful for his partner's quick reflexes and fantastic luck.

"...That was a close one...," he gasped, forcing himself to his feet.

Up on the landing, the Integrity Knight seemed at a loss. His quiver was empty, and the string of his bow hung limp and broken. There could be no greater loss for an archer. But this was an Integrity Knight, not someone to underestimate and certainly not one to pity.

"...Let's go," Eugeo murmured, taking a step up.

But Kirito thrust out a hand to stop him, still holding the arrow he'd pulled from his shoe. "Wait...The knight is casting a sacred art..."

"Huh?"

Eugeo paused to listen. Since they were outside of attack range, they needed to respond to any spell with one of the opposite element. He focused on the voice coming through the knight's metal helmet. The chanting pace was speedy, but thanks to the study they'd done in the library, he could make out the words.

Yet the art itself was unfamiliar to him. Without hearing the *Generate* command that would identify the type of element being summoned, there was no way to counteract it effectively.

"Uh-oh, this is bad," Kirito moaned. "It's not an elemental art, it's Perfect Weapon Control."

No sooner was the statement out of his mouth than the knight finished, clear and crisp, with "Enhance Armament!"

The two ends of the snapped string suddenly lit up with orange flame, accompanied by the soft sound of their ignition. The fire burned through the string in an instant, and when it reached the ends of the longbow, the copper-colored weapon burst into roiling red flame.

Even at the bottom of the staircase, Eugeo had to turn his face away from the skin-searing heat. The fire shooting from the bow wreathed the Integrity Knight himself, making it seem like he was aflame.

This development caught Eugeo by such surprise that he was unsure how to react. Should he assume that even with Perfect Weapon Control, the lack of any arrows was a major loss of power and charge in? Or was using up all his arrows at once a sign that the knight knew he didn't *need* any more arrows with his bow in this state?

Eugeo glanced briefly at his partner to see how he was reacting. Kirito was neither pulling back nor charging forward, but staring wide-eyed with a childlike grin on his lips.

"This is amazing…I wonder what that bow was made of originally."

"Now's not the time for that!" Eugeo said, resisting the urge to punch his friend's shoulder. They could choose to use their newly learned Perfect Control to fight back, but their opponent would not wait for them—he would certainly attack before they could complete the long chant. If they were going to use that, they needed to have started it at the same time as he.

Eugeo prepared himself to react when the enemy struck, but the knight decided to pause, transferring his blazing bow to one hand so he could lift his helmet visor with the other.

His face was hidden in the shadows cast by the flames, but Eugeo could sense a steely gaze just as sharp as those arrows. The knight's voice was so hard it scarcely seemed human.

"It has been two years since I last bathed in the fire of my Conflagration Bow. I can see that you have the skill to match Eldrie Synthesis Thirty-One indeed, sinners. Now your crimes have further deepened. You did not best him in proper combat but misled him with the impure dark arts!"

"D-dark arts?" Kirito gaped.

Eugeo was equally taken aback, and he shook his head in denial. "N-no! We didn't use any dark magic! We just talked about the time before Eldrie became an Integrity Knight..."

"*Before* he became a knight?! We have no past! The shining Integrity Knights are all we have ever been after our summoning from Heaven!!" he belted, voice echoing like steel off the staircase.

Eugeo held his breath. Cardinal had told them that the Integrity Knights couldn't access their preknighthood memories. So this red knight had been led to believe that he, too, was summoned from the heavenly realm.

If they could stimulate the memories being blocked by his Piety Module, they could shake this man, too, but that was impossible given that they didn't even know his name. They couldn't stop him in his tracks the same way they did with Eldrie.

Standing amid a sea of airborne sparks from his bow, the knight barked like a bolt of lightning. "I have been ordered to take you alive, so I cannot reduce you to ash, but now that I have unleashed the power of the Conflagration Bow, know that you are likely to lose an arm or two! Let us see if you can evade the flames of condemnation and reach me with your flimsy blades!"

He held his bow aloft and placed his right hand in the spot where the drawstring should have been. His fingers pinched shut, but there was nothing there. It couldn't mean—

Fierce flames ran out in front of the bow, shifting into the shape of an arrow. The burning red projectile gleamed with tremendous power. Eugeo felt his spine stiffen.

"No string, no ammo, no problem," Kirito muttered.

Eugeo turned to him, chin nearly quivering, and asked, "Do you have a plan?"

"I have to believe that he can't shoot consecutively. I'll find some way to stop that first shot, and then you hack away at him."

"You...'believe'...?"

Meaning that if he can shoot those flame arrows one after the other, we're done for. But even if it's just the one, wouldn't that mean it's enough to finish us off without a follow-up? How does Kirito plan to defend against it? Eugeo wondered, but there was no time left for that now.

"All right," he agreed. If Kirito said he could stop it, he would. This was still far more realistic than when he said he'd chop down the Gigas Cedar.

The two readied their swords and showed signs of determination, prompting the Integrity Knight to pull back on his invisible string.

The heat licking at Eugeo's cheeks strengthened. The flames from the Conflagration Bow were soaring up to the ceiling over the landing, painting the marble surface black.

Kirito's movement was sudden. He charged without a yell, without a grand launching leap, like a leaf caught in a rapid river. One breath later, Eugeo hurried after him.

As they climbed, he noticed a faint blue light leaking from his partner's left hand where it loosely held the sword. Eugeo would never mistake the tint of a frost element, which he must have generated while the knight was giving his speech.

By the time they were halfway up the twenty-step staircase, the knight had the bow drawn to its full length. That was when a high-speed stream of commands burst from Kirito's mouth. "Form Element, Shield Shape! Discharge!"

He thrust out his left hand, hurling a line of five elements, the maximum that one hand could generate at a time. The blue points formed a line of large round shields, one after the other, that filled the space between Kirito and the Integrity Knight.

The knight barked yet again. "Laughable! Pierce him!!"

With a roar like the breath from a fire dragon, the arrow—more like a spear—of flame launched itself forward.

It took only an instant for the flaming spear to intersect with Kirito's ice shield line.

The first shield burst easily, the shards instantly evaporating into steam.

The second and third erupted before the sound even reached their ears.

The fourth shield softened and warped in the middle where the arrow landed, but it still burst. Through the final shield, the flaming lance bore down, filling the entire scene with red.

Throughout it all, Eugeo kept his pace going up the stairs. He couldn't slow down now while his partner maintained that mad dash.

As Eugeo watched, teeth gritted, the fiery spear made contact with the fifth shield and finally slowed its ferocious pace just a bit. Sparks shot through the air as the projectile sought to shatter its obstacle of the opposing element.

"——?!"

Eugeo's eyes bulged. For an instant, it looked like the fiery spear changed shape on the other side of the translucent ice wall. It sprouted a large beak and spread wings, like some great bird of prey...

But before he could so much as blink, the final shield cracked and burst.

Blazing heat washed over him, drying the breath from his lungs. The spear of fire, the phoenix, hurtled down on Kirito, free of all the barriers at last.

"*Yaaaah!!*"

At last, a fierce shout burst from Kirito's throat. He thrust his black sword forward.

Surely he isn't going to try to cut that bird, Eugeo thought. Instead, Kirito's extended blade traced an unexpected path. Faster than the eye could follow, it spun like a windmill around the axle of his glowing fingers.

But the speed of rotation was abnormal. However he was managing to spin his fingers, the blade was moving fast enough to be a blur, as if it, too, was now a translucent shield blocking the way.

The head of the phoenix made contact with the sixth shield.

There was a fierce blasting sound, perhaps a roar of fury from the bird—and then the flaming projectile that had pierced five shields of ice was torn into scattering shreds by the spinning blade. More than a little of it landed on Kirito, and the pieces caused small explosions where they hit.

Eugeo saw his partner's body fly through the air as though struck, and he screamed. "Kiriiito!!"

Even through the shower of sparks and flames, Kirito managed to shout back. "Don't stop, Eugeo!!"

His momentary hesitation gone, Eugeo stared ahead. Kirito would never halt and give up that one sliver of hope in this situation. He did what he said he would. Now it was Eugeo's turn.

He practically flew up the steps, passing the airborne body of his partner to the right. Once he was through the last remnants of floating fire, the landing and the Integrity Knight standing on it were right before him.

Surely the knight wouldn't expect that one could escape his mighty Perfect Weapon Control attack unscathed. His face was still hidden in the helmet, even at this range, but Eugeo thought he sensed surprise. There wasn't enough time for a second projectile. He had no sword, and he had allowed his foe to reach close quarters.

Now you've lost! Eugeo thought triumphantly, raising the Blue Rose Sword high.

"Toy with me not, boy!!" the knight bellowed, reading Eugeo's mind.

Whatever momentary surprise he felt was gone, and pure fighting fury enveloped the heavy reddish armor. He held his left hand high overhead, still clutching the burning longbow, and flame burst around his fist again.

"*Daaah!!*" he screamed, hurtling his fist forward through the burning air.

What now?!

Eugeo was already in slicing range, but a series of calculations spun through his head at the speed of light.

It was fist versus sword, so in terms of range and power, he had the advantage. But his opponent had the advantage of terrain. He was already very tall, and his fist was coming from an added height advantage of three extra steps. Could the slender Blue Rose Sword withstand that kind of power? Should he dodge sideways, take the landing, and then attack again?

No. Eugeo's friend and master in the Aincrad style had once told him, *In this world, what you put into your sword is crucial. And it's up to you to find what you infuse into your blade.*

Eugeo's tutor, Golgorosso; Kirito's tutor, Sortiliena; and even the arrogant and cowardly nobles Raios and Humbert had *something* that gave their swords added power. But Eugeo could sense that he was still in the process of finding that thing for himself. He had trained as much as anyone and learned a number of advanced techniques, but he still hadn't found what he could put into his sword to make it stand apart. He wasn't born to be a swordsman; perhaps he would never find it.

But at this moment, he couldn't submit to the Integrity Knight's intensity and allow his weapon to shrink back. The time for training and building his skill was gone. Now was the time to achieve his goal. Now was the time to take back the old Alice from her new Integrity Knight form.

Alice.

That was the only thing that mattered. He'd watched his friend get dragged away in chains that summer day eight years ago, and now was the time to save her at last. All of his sword training and sacred arts knowledge was for this very moment.

Please, give me your strength. I still have so much to learn, and I might not be fit to own a sword of your pedigree…but I can't stop and pull back now!

With the Blue Rose Sword high, Eugeo twisted himself even farther backward. The slightly translucent blade took on a brilliant blue glow, denoting the Aincrad style's Vertical attack.

"Aaaah!" he bellowed, and then he swung. The sword sizzled forward with that special sound unique to ultimate techniques and collided with the burning fist of the Integrity Knight.

The shock wave of blue and red light fanned out, tearing the red carpet on the steps and the woven tapestries on the walls. Fist and sword came to a stop, connected in midair.

The gauntlet and the flat of the blade creaked. Eugeo summoned all his strength in the hopes of finishing the technique, but the knight's arm was as immobile as a boulder—although he did not seem to be overpowering the sword, either. A low growl emerged from the helmet, and more weight was added to his fist.

But the stalemate lasted only a few seconds. The flame coming from the Conflagration Bow in the knight's hand started to lick at the Blue Rose Sword. The light along the blade began to flicker, as if wilting under the heat. If his Vertical faltered, his sword would be knocked aside to give him a face full of burning fist.

"Grr...uuaagh...!"

Eugeo summoned all the strength and willpower he had in an attempt to swing through. But the flames only grew in strength. The blade began to heat up, turning red.

Though he'd never been conscious of it before, the memories of the sword that he saw in the Great Library said that the Blue Rose Sword had ice properties. That meant it should be weak to powerful flames, as its opposing element. If this continued for much longer, it could sap a dangerous amount of life from the weapon.

But on the flip side, the element of the sword meant it could possibly overcome the enemy's flames, as well.

You've been forged in the freezing storms at the peak of the End Mountains since the days of the world's creation. Don't let this cheap little fire melt you now! Eugeo screamed in his mind.

The sword responded. Instantly, both his main hand on the grip and his left supporting the pommel felt a stinging chill. It wasn't just his imagination—the little roses carved into the guard were shrouded in white frost. The frost advanced, growing into little vines that crawled up the blade and scattered the flames licking at it.

The phenomenon didn't stop there. The white vines of ice grew onto the knight's fist where it touched the sword, banishing the flames that covered the red gauntlet and spreading more frost…

"Hrrng…," the knight grunted, surprised at the sudden chill. The moment that Eugeo sensed his opponent's stance was faltering, he unleashed all the strength he'd been building.

With an ear-ripping squeal, the sword plunged forward and pushed the knight's left gauntlet back. Unfortunately, the tip just missed the enemy's body. As the sword descended through air, the knight threw his empty right fist at Eugeo. It wasn't flaming like the other one, but a solid blow from that rock-hard fist would easily knock him back to the base of the stairs.

But Eugeo let out a fierce cry, and his sword leaped upward.

"Iyaaaah!"

Even the burliest of men couldn't perform an instantaneous reversal of momentum with strength alone—not when the Blue Rose Sword was heavier than a steel sword of the same size. Only a swordfighting technique could achieve such an effect: the Aincrad style's two-part attack, Vertical Arc.

The blade traced a figure like the sacred arts rune V, slicing into the Integrity Knight's breastplate at an angle. A small amount of red liquid sprayed from the gash in the dark-red metal. The tip of his sword had tasted flesh—but only a bit.

The knight swayed backward, but he tensed his legs to leap away. If Eugeo let the enemy gain any distance, it would give him a chance to repeat his flame attack. But all of the Aincrad style's ultimate techniques left the user immobilized for several seconds after finishing.

Kirito told him that if he was going to use them, he always had to consider how he would make up for that massive period of weakness. If the attack landed effectively, it wasn't an issue, but if it was blocked or deflected—or, as in this case, it landed but didn't fully stop the opponent—he would be open to the risk of a fatal counterattack.

The immobilization of a technique was absolute; no amount of mental fortitude could lessen it. The only ways to minimize the risk were tricks like having an ally step in afterward or unleashing prepared wind elements to blow the enemy farther away, and so on. But Kirito had fallen back down into the antechamber, and there hadn't been time to chant any sacred arts. There was only one way left.

Eugeo summoned all the muscle and willpower he had to control the movement of the Blue Rose Sword along the route of the second half of its Vertical Arc. Normally it would end up high to the left, but instead he brought it back so that it practically rested on his left shoulder. Forcing the blade aside caused the blue light surrounding it to diminish rapidly, but the attack was essentially over anyway.

Just as the Blue Rose Sword came to a stop over his shoulder, the enemy knight leaped into motion. The landing of the staircase was spacious, and if he retreated toward the back wall, he could likely prepare another flaming lance while Eugeo was paralyzed. If Eugeo let that happen, he could not defend against it.

The final way to overcome the momentary paralysis was to stitch one ultimate technique into another. If the posture at the end of one attack matched the initiation of another, it could segue smoothly without causing any delay. This ultimate art of technique combination was so difficult, even Kirito could only pull it off half the time.

"...Hah!!"

Eugeo belted hot breath and focused as hard as he could on activating the new technique. The sword shone brightly, his body bolted forward as if struck, and the sword roared forward from the upper left toward the Integrity Knight. It was the singular attack move Slant.

At last, the knight's eyes bulged.

The pain in Eugeo's right eye and the rotating red sacred letters from when he tried to attack Raios were gone. There was no feeling of doubt, no hesitation whatsoever. Eugeo's entire being was driven by one thought only: to slice the foe before him.

The Blue Rose Sword struck the knight directly on the right shoulder. The shoulder guard split, followed by a dull, heavy impact that traveled up to Eugeo's hand. It was the sensation of the sword in his hand splitting muscle and flesh to crush bone.

The Integrity Knight was slammed directly to the floor on his back, wounded deeply from shoulder to breast.

"Gakh!" he gasped, voice muffled by the helmet, and then a spray of blood redder than his armor burst from the neck of his suit.

This was the second time Eugeo had slashed a man, and he still felt his breath catch in his throat for a moment. The sensation in his right hand caused something to clutch at the pit of his stomach, but he did his best to suppress it.

In a kind of coordination with Eugeo's emotions, the Blue Rose Sword exuded frost again, turning all the blood on it into ice that vanished, leaving it clean. In fact, the wound on the knight's shoulder was also white with frost now, the captured drops of blood hardening into little icicles.

"Rrgh...," the knight grunted, lifting his left hand with the bow toward his wound. Eugeo clenched his sword harder again—if the Integrity Knight started some kind of sacred art, he would have to strike him again. An experienced caster could heal himself with all the available resources in the vicinity, and the only ways to stop him were to attack his throat, cut off his arm—or perhaps end his life altogether.

But the knight's left fist was totally frozen, and when he realized that he could not even let go of the bow, he gave up on healing himself. Element-based sacred arts required fine finger movement to execute. Instead, he exhaled in chagrin and dropped his arm heavily to the floor.

Eugeo wasn't sure what to do next. The Blue Rose Sword's ice effect stopped the enemy's flame in its tracks, but it also sealed the wound and stopped the bleeding. The knight couldn't fight back for now, but he wouldn't die, either. If left here, his hand would eventually thaw, and then he could heal himself and possibly continue pursuing them.

All Eugeo could do was stand in place and grit his teeth in indecision. It was the knight who spoke first.

"...Boy..."

Even in a rasp, his voice lost none of its commanding presence. Eugeo tensed at first, until he heard what came next.

"What is the name of the first technique you used...?"

"..."

Eugeo hesitated at first, then opened his parched lips to answer, "...The Aincrad-style two-part combination, Vertical Arc."

"Two...part," the knight repeated, pausing, then asked, "And you...what did *you* do...?"

His helmet creaked, and for an instant Eugeo looked behind him. There was Kirito, black clothes singed here and there, holding his left arm and dragging his right foot as he slowly ascended the stairs.

"Kirito...are you hurt?!"

His partner grinned weakly. "I'm fine. I already took care of the worst burns. Sir Knight, what I performed was the Aincrad-style defensive maneuver Spinning Shield."

"..."

The knight looked up at the ceiling, helmet clanking, and fell silent. When he spoke again after several seconds, it seemed to be directed at himself rather than Eugeo or Kirito.

"...I have been from one edge of the human world to the other...and even seen what lies beyond...but now I have learned that there are techniques and styles in the world that are yet unfamiliar to me...I can sense that there is true discipline and experience in your style. When I accused you of using defiled arts to lead Eldrie astray...it seems that I was mistaken."

His helmet creaked again as he turned to stare at Eugeo from within the helmet. "...Tell me...your names."

Eugeo glanced at Kirito, then said, "...Eugeo the swordsman. I have no second name."

"I am Kirito the swordsman."

The knight nodded, savoring the sound, and then, to their surprise, said, "...Several Integrity Knights are awaiting you in the Great Hall of Ghostly Light on the fiftieth floor of the cathedral. They are under orders to obliterate your life rather than take you alive, however...So if you attempt to challenge them directly, they will instantly destroy you."

"Whoa...Buddy, should you really be telling us that?" Kirito interjected.

But the knight seemed to grin (as far as could be seen with his helmet on) and muttered, "Having failed to fulfill my duty as given by Administrator...my knight's armor and weapon will surely be confiscated, and I will undergo an eternal freezing... So before I suffer that ignominious fate, I would prefer...that you end my life yourselves."

"..."

Eugeo and Kirito could not respond. The knight continued, "There is no reason to hesitate...You defeated me through skill and boldness, in fair combat..."

But any surprise Eugeo had felt was soon washed away by his formal introduction.

"My name...is Deusolbert Synthesis Seven."

It was more than just familiar.

That was a name that had been etched deep into Eugeo's soul for the past eight years, a name he could never forget for an instant. A name that conjured up regret, despair, and anger.

"Deusol...bert? You...*you* were the knight who...?"

To his own ears, Eugeo's hoarse voice sounded like it belonged to someone else. The color of the armor was different, and the metallic muffling of the voice through the helmet had given away nothing. But now he understood that the knight on the floor before him was the very one who...

Eugeo staggered forward, compelled.

"Eugeo...?" said Kirito, but the brown-haired boy hardly even heard it. He leaned over to look at the face through the helmet visor.

There was some kind of enchantment on the helmet, because from just a few dozen cens away, the knight's face was still hidden in darkness. But even after the loss of so much of his life value, his two eyes were clearly visible, having lost none of their force.

They were sharp and bold and could have belonged to either a young man or an experienced one.

Eugeo's voice creaked out of his parched throat. "End...your life...? Fair combat...?"

His right hand spasmed violently, and the sword clutched in it began to radiate cold once again. The armor right under the tip began to freeze over in white.

A ball of furious hot rage swelled up inside him, and he forced it out with one throat-ripping accusation.

"You shackled a girl...who was only eleven—*eleven years old!*—and chained her to the foot of a dragon...and you think you have the right to take the *honorable* way out?!"

He held up the Blue Rose Sword in reverse, the blade pointed down.

He would ram it through that knight's mouth and his unforgivable words, right down to the floor, and be done with it.

But a heavy, wincing pain stayed his hand. The pain didn't come from his right eye but somewhere deep in his chest. It was the pain of someone, somewhere, desperately trying to stop him.

He stood there, sword raised, entire body trembling with emotion—until Kirito reached over to put his hand on Eugeo's arm.

"......Why...are you...stopping me, Kirito...?" he ground out to his partner, the person he trusted more than anyone in the world, as he grappled with a maelstrom of emotion that threatened to consume his entire sense of reason.

Kirito stared back at him with eyes full of pain and slowly shook his head.

"This man doesn't intend to fight anymore. You shouldn't use your sword on someone who won't fight..."

"But...but he...he was the one who took Alice away...He...," Eugeo protested, like a sulking child, but a part of him knew that Kirito was right.

The Integrity Knights were beings who acted entirely on the commands of the Axiom Church—the pontifex herself. It was the *Church*, the twisted law and order that ruled over the world, that took Alice away.

But even taking a step back did not rid him of the impulse to forget all about the truth and simply slice the prone knight to pieces. Learning the way the world really worked didn't simply wipe clean the years of anger, powerlessness, and guilt that had built up since that fateful summer day.

A woven basket at his feet. Bread and cheese lying in the sand. Ice melting in the sun.

The dull shine of the chains that bound Alice's blue dress. And his two feet, as immobile as if they'd grown roots on the spot.

…Kirito…Kirito.

If you had been there, you would have attacked the knight to save Alice, if that's what it took. You would have done it, even knowing that you'd be arrested and subjected to interrogation, too.

But I couldn't do it. Alice was my one true friend, the girl I cared about more than anyone else, and all I could do was watch. All I could do was watch as this knight on the ground here tied her up and took her away.

His mind was a storm, fragments of emotions and thoughts coming and going. His arm trembled in Kirito's grasp and lifted the sword even higher.

But what Kirito said next was stunning enough that it succeeded at stopping Eugeo.

"…I don't think he remembers that. He doesn't remember taking your Alice away from Rulid…and not because he forgot but because the memory was erased."

"Huh…?"

Stunned, Eugeo looked down at the knight's helmet.

The Integrity Knight, who hadn't budged once, even with the sword held over his head, finally moved. His left fist, thawed at last, pried itself open and let go of the longbow in a spray of little ice shards. He reached up to undo the fasteners of his helmet.

The menacing metal structure split in the front and back, then clattered free from the knight's head. It revealed the fierce, stern face of a man who appeared to be around forty.

He had close-cropped hair and thick brows, both a burnished

red color like rust. The bridge of his nose and the line of his mouth were straight and proud, and his eyes were as sharp as steel arrowheads.

But those dark eyes were wavering, betraying an internal struggle. His thin lips parted to produce a deep, rich voice that sounded nothing like what had come through the helmet.

"...This black-haired boy...is correct. You claim that I chained a young girl and brought her here by dragon? I do not remember such a thing."

"You...you don't remember...? It was only eight years ago," Eugeo murmured, stunned. The tension drained from his arm. Kirito removed his hand from Eugeo and put it to his chin, thinking hard.

"That's why it was erased...along with everything before and after. Hey, guy...er, Sir Deusolbert, were you the Integrity Knight in charge of protecting the north border of Norlangarth?"

"...Indeed. Norlangarth North District Seven was...under my jurisdiction. Up until eight years ago," the knight said, his brows furrowing as he dredged up memories. "And then...in recognition of my feats...I was given this armor...and placed in a security role at Central Cathedral..."

"Do you remember what feat it was?" Kirito asked. The knight did not answer immediately. He pursed his lips, and his eyes wandered. After a short silence, Kirito continued, "I'll tell you why. Your feat was finding the Integrity Knight Alice Synthesis Thirty—from a tiny little frontier hamlet in the far north that no one in Centoria would have known about. Administrator gave you credit for bringing Alice to this tower but also had to remove your memories of the event...and you just explained the reason why."

At some point, Kirito had stopped talking to Eugeo and the knight and seemed to be laying out his argument for himself as his speech accelerated.

"You said that the Integrity Knights have no past, because you were summoned from Heaven. I'm sure that's what the pontifex told you just after you awoke as a knight, in order to convince you that you had no memories before then. But in order to maintain that story, there had to be no memories, not just of *your* humanity but of the birth of any other knights. After all, there would be chaos if the sinner you brought to justice showed up as an Integrity Knight the next day. I suppose that might actually be the pontifex's biggest weakness..."

Kirito looked down, pacing left and right, pondering at a rapid pace. This outburst by his partner sapped the momentum of Eugeo's fury. He looked down at the man at his feet again. Deusolbert's face was similarly vacant as he considered these ramifications.

His anger and hatred weren't gone, but if Kirito was correct that all of the man's memories of Alice had been erased, then perhaps Eugeo just had to accept the state of things: that all the Integrity Knights were merely pawns of this Administrator at the center of the Axiom Church. The true enemy who stole Alice from him, and turned her into a knight and erased her memories, was none other than the Administrator.

Deusolbert, sensing Eugeo's gaze upon him, stopped glancing around. It was impossible to tell what exact emotions were swirling within the older man, but when his voice emerged at last, it wavered with a weakness that would be unthinkable from the imposing figure they'd faced in battle.

"That...cannot be...We Integrity Knights cannot have been human beings like you...before our knighting..."

"..."

Eugeo was at a loss for words. Instead, Kirito spoke for him.

"The blood from your wound is the same red as ours. And Eldrie wasn't acting strange because we cast some wicked art on him. It was because we were trying to make him remember the memories that were taken from him...And you're no different from him. I don't know whether you won the Four-Empire Unification Tournament or committed some sin according to the Taboo Index, but in either case, Administrator took important memories of yours, forced absolute loyalty to the Church into your soul, and turned you into an Integrity Knight. Whatever this freezing punishment is, I'm certain that Administrator will just tinker with your memories again and erase this conversation. I'd bet on it."

His phrasing was cold, but there was a kind of helpless frustration in Kirito's voice, too. Picking up on that, the knight closed his eyes and then eventually shook his head.

"I cannot believe. I cannot believe that the holy pontifex... would do such a thing to me..."

"But it's the truth. There *must* be something still left in you. A precious memory from before you became a knight that no sacred arts can wipe from your mind..."

Deusolbert lifted his left hand, stared at the thick, strong fingers, and exhaled. "From the time I first came to earth...I have had the same dream, over and over...of a small hand rocking me awake...and a silver ring on its finger...But when I wake...there is no one there..."

His brows furrowed, and he pressed hard against his forehead. Kirito watched him solemnly, then murmured, "I don't think you *can* remember any more than that. Administrator stole your memory of whoever owned that ring..."

He paused, then returned the black sword in his hand to the sheath at his left side with a soft *clink*. "...What you do next is up to you. You can return to Administrator and receive your punishment, heal up, and chase after us...or..."

Kirito left the final option unsaid and took a few steps toward the next flight of stairs on the right end of the landing. He paused there and looked over his shoulder, straight at Eugeo.

His black eyes were saying, *Isn't that better?* Eugeo glanced down at the prone Integrity Knight, whose eyes were closed. He lifted the Blue Rose Sword, then pointed the tip at his sheath and slid it home.

"...Let's go," he said, pulling even with Kirito, and they began to climb together.

Whatever choice Deusolbert Synthesis Seven made, it seemed unlikely that he would pursue them after this.

2

For quite a while after that, the only sound was of boot soles striking marble stairs.

Everything else was ear-splitting silence. As far as Eugeo knew, there were many monks and understudies living in the Axiom Church's central building, but no matter how they looked and listened, there was no sign of life anywhere around them.

On top of that, the sight that confronted them on each new floor—a rectangular chamber with hallways extending forward and to the sides, with equally spaced doors along them—was so uniform that it began to feel like they were under some kind of bewitching spell that was making them pass the same exact floor, over and over again.

Eugeo wanted to stop and check a nearby door on one of the floors, just to confirm that this wasn't the case, but Kirito's upward progress was so steady that it seemed like a bad idea to disrupt him. If Deusolbert was telling them the truth, the fiftieth floor not too much farther up would feature many more foes to deal with.

He ran his fingertips along the hilt of the sword at his side to calm his mind and focus on the task at hand.

Just then, Kirito came to a sudden stop on the staircase landing just ahead. He turned back, face dead serious, and said, "Hey, Eugeo.........What floor are we on now...?"

"Um...well," Eugeo said, wobbling a bit. He sighed, shook his head, and slumped his shoulders all at the same time. "Next one's the twenty-ninth floor. I'm going to assume you were at least counting at the start."

"Well, you'd think they would have floor number displays along the way. I mean, it's just common sense."

"I agree, but you should have noticed before this!" Eugeo scolded, but Kirito merely brushed it off and rested his back against the landing wall.

"So we're still only that far up...I was sure we were way farther. Man, I'm getting hungry..."

"...I agree with you there."

It had been nearly five hours since their fancy breakfast with Cardinal in the library. Through the long, narrow windows, Solus appeared to be near its peak. And after a fierce battle, followed by twenty-five flights of stairs (a thousand steps in total), it was natural that their bodies were asking for replenishment.

Eugeo thrust out his hand and demanded, "So hand over one of the ones you've got in your pockets."

"Uh...but...I was saving them for emergencies...Man, you're greedier than I thought."

"You thought I wouldn't notice how much you stuffed in there?"

Kirito gave up and slipped his right hand into his pants pocket, then pulled out two steamed buns and handed one to Eugeo. The smell of it was still strong enough to stimulate his appetite, even though they'd left the library long ago.

"That flame attack kinda charred it a bit."

"Ha-ha...I see. Thanks, man."

Cardinal had generated the steamed bun out of some precious old tome's pages using her high-level sacred arts, a fact that Eugeo had to ignore as he bit into the treat. The crispy, burned outside gave way to juicy meat on the inside, which he savored rapturously.

In less than a minute, their little lunch was over, and Eugeo licked his fingers in satisfaction. Kirito's other pocket was still bulging suspiciously, but Eugeo was happy enough to let it go for now.

"Thanks for the meal. So, what now? We should reach the fiftieth floor in another thirty minutes or so. Do we just charge straight up there?"

"Hmm..." Kirito grunted, scratching his head. "Good question...I think we've seen firsthand how deadly a fight against the Integrity Knights can be, but on the other hand, if we're taking the fight between you and him as an example, they don't seem to have much experience facing combination attacks, if any. I want to believe we stand a chance in a close-range, one-on-one battle. But if there are multiple knights ready and waiting, that becomes much more difficult."

"So...we give up on charging straight through and find another way instead?"

"I'm not sure about that, either. Cardinal said this staircase was the only way up, and even if we find some kind of shortcut, it still leaves the possibility that we'll get ambushed. I really think we need to beat those Integrity Knights on the fiftieth floor while we're there. We're going to be forced to use the ace up our sleeve, but thanks to the warning he gave us, we know we'll have time to prepare those long commands before we get there."

"Oh, right...the Perfect Weapon Control," Eugeo murmured.

"I'm worried about using it for the first time in an actual battle," Kirito admitted, "but it doesn't make sense to test it here and waste our swords' durability, either. We should use our Perfect Control right as we're reaching the fiftieth floor and neutralize as many knights as we can..."

"Uh, Kirito, about that...," Eugeo said, feeling bad about bringing it up. "Um...my Perfect Control isn't going to be a powerful direct attack—not like that knight's just now."

"Huh? It's...not?"

"Well, it was Cardinal who wrote my actual command. I mean, I know it was *me* who envisioned the actual thing," Eugeo said, feeling apologetic.

Mildly confused, Kirito suggested, "Why don't you try reciting it now? Just don't include the starter command."

"Okay."

Eugeo rattled off the various parts of the long command, leaving out the System Call that was supposed to precede them all. Kirito listened with his eyes closed, and after Eugeo finished with *Enhance Armament*, he had a surprising smile on his lips.

"I see. You're right; it's not exactly offensive in nature, but it can be plenty helpful if we use it properly. And it seems like it should complement my own pretty well."

"Really? What kind is yours?"

"Why ruin the surprise now?" Kirito teased, earning himself a glare from Eugeo. He swept his bangs aside with a smug smile and leaned against the wall again. "Okay, I think I know what we'll do, not that it's much of a plan. First, before we exit onto the fiftieth floor, we chant our Perfect Weapon Control and keep it on standby. Once we're in there and know where our enemies are, you unleash first, and I'll go after. If we manage to successfully cluster the knights in one spot, we might be able to neutralize them all at once."

"*Might*," Eugeo repeated with plenty of skepticism. But in truth, he had no countersuggestion. Admittedly, his partner was the better one when it came to planning with all possible variables in mind, and given Eugeo's trouble with high-speed chanting, the chance to take care of it beforehand was greatly appreciated.

"...So let's go with that. First, I'll..."

Eugeo turned to his left and glanced at the staircase leading up to the twenty-ninth floor of the cathedral. Then his eyes bulged.

In the shadows beneath the handrail were two small heads and two pairs of eyes watching them intently.

The instant Eugeo's gaze passed over them, the heads darted back behind cover. But even as he watched, momentarily stunned, they eventually came back into view, innocent eyes blinking with interest.

Kirito sensed the anomaly and followed Eugeo's line of sight. His mouth, too, fell open, before he finally asked, "Uh...who are you?"

The two heads shared a look, then a little bob, and then the bodies attached came into view.

"They're...children?" Eugeo couldn't help but mutter.

Standing on the stairs were two girls, dressed in identical black outfits. They looked to be around ten. Eugeo felt a flash of fond reminiscence and then realized it was because their plain black clothes looked a little bit like the apprentice habit that Alice's sister, Selka, wore back at the church in Rulid.

But unlike Selka, these girls had green belts with thirty-cen swords attached. For an instant, he felt his hackles rise, but just as soon, he noticed that the blades and hilts were made of reddish wood. While the coloring was different, they looked just like the little wooden swords every child used to practice.

The girl on the right had her light-brown hair tied into two braids. Her eyebrows sloped downward over her round eyes, giving her a weak-willed look. The girl on the left had straw-blond hair cut short, and her eyes were sharp and triumphant.

To no surprise, the first of the two to step forward was the bolder-looking one on the left. She took a deep breath and abruptly introduced herself.

"Um...I'm Fizel, an Axiom Church sister-in-training. And she's another apprentice like me..."

"L...Linel."

Their youthful voices wavered a bit at the end due to nerves. Eugeo smiled to put them at ease, but then he realized that if they were holy women in the Church—even as apprentices—that made them enemies.

But Fizel's follow-up question was even more direct than Eugeo's line of thought.

"Um...are *you* the intruders from the Dark Territory?"

"Huh...?"

He and Kirito shared a look. Even his partner seemed at a loss for how to respond. His mouth opened and shut several times without producing any words, and then he drew himself behind Eugeo and said, "I'm not good with kids. You take this one."

Eugeo hissed, "No fair!" but he couldn't circle around to hide behind Kirito. Instead, he looked up at the two girls and said awkwardly, "Um...well, uh...we're from the human world, actually... but I guess if anyone's an intruder, it would be us..."

The girls put their heads together and started trading whispers. Their voices were low, but the area was so devastatingly quiet that they couldn't help but be audible at this distance.

"See? They look like totally normal humans, Nel. No horns or tails!" hissed Fizel, the feistier of the two.

The other one, Linel, argued, "I—I just told you that was in the book, that's all. You're the one who took the idea and ran with it, Zel."

"Hmm. Maybe they're just hiding them. Would we be able to tell if we got closer?"

"But they just look like totally normal people. Then again... they could have fangs in their mouths..."

Eugeo couldn't stifle a grin, as he was reminded of Telure and Teline, the twin girls from Walde Farm. If he and Kirito were that age and had heard about intruders from the land of darkness nearby, they would have very likely tried to go see them, too. And they'd probably have gotten a tongue-lashing from their father or the village elder for it.

That thought gave Eugeo pause. What if the girls got punished for making contact with rebels against the Church? It didn't seem like he was in a position to spend much time worrying about that, but he couldn't help himself.

"Um...are you girls going to get in trouble for talking to us?"

Fizel and Linel both went silent and then grinned. Fizel replied with a smirk and considerably less formality than before. "This morning, all the monks, nuns, and apprentices were ordered to stay in their rooms and lock the doors. Don't you get it? We can slip out to see the intruders, and no one's going to be around to notice us."

"Uh...right..."

It was just the kind of logic that Kirito would come up with. In fact, he could practically see his partner getting scolded for it already.

The girls discussed something between themselves again, and this time, it was Linel who said, "Um…and you're definitely not monsters from the Dark Territory?"

"N-no."

"Then, if you don't mind, may we see you up close? Um…your forehead and teeth in particular."

"Huh?" Eugeo replied, turning around to Kirito for help, but the other boy was conveniently looking away. This one would be up to Eugeo.

"…Well…I suppose that would be all right…"

The inability to refuse such a request was in his nature, but a part of Eugeo also felt it was important for people to realize that even a traitor like him was a regular human being. Plus, they might be able to get information about the cathedral from the girls.

Their faces shining, Fizel and Linel trotted over with a mixture of curiosity and caution. They stopped when they reached the landing and stared with blue and gray eyes.

Eugeo crouched over, drew back his bangs from his forehead, and showed them his teeth. They stared at him without blinking for a good ten seconds, then looked satisfied.

"He's human."

"Yes, human."

He snorted at the obvious disappointment in their reaction. Linel wondered, "But if you're not monsters from the Dark Territory, why did you decide to infiltrate Central Cathedral?"

"Um, well…," Eugeo started, wondering how they could continually throw him off guard, then decided to be honest and admitted, "…Long ago, a little girl who was a friend of mine got taken away by an Integrity Knight. So I'm here to take her back."

Surely, this statement would be difficult to accept, given how a sister-in-training would feel about the righteousness of the Axiom Church. Eugeo expected to see fear and revulsion in their young features, but instead, they merely bobbed their heads.

Fizel, the one with the straw-blond hair, complained, "Oh. That's kind of an ordinary reason."

"O-ordinary?"

"People whose families or lovers have been taken here have always come to argue their case to the Church. Not many, but it happens. But I bet you two are the first who actually got all the way inside."

Linel continued, "Plus, you got thrown into prison, and yet you broke your spiritual chains, then you defeated two Integrity Knights. So we figured you were monsters…maybe even real dark knights. And it turns out you're just ordinary humans…"

The girls looked at each other and said, "Good enough?" "Good enough."

Linel turned to Eugeo again and tilted her head at a questioning angle, braids swaying. "Well, can you at least tell us your names, here at the end?"

Surprised, because he was hoping to ask them plenty of his own questions, Eugeo replied, "I'm Eugeo. And that's Kirito behind me."

"Oh…No last names?"

"Er, no. I was raised out on the frontier…Same for you two?"

"No, we have full names," said Linel, smiling. It was the bright innocent smile of one about to stuff her face with a delicious treat.

"My name is Linel Synthesis Twenty-Eight."

In the moment, Eugeo could not process the implication of that name.

Suddenly, he felt a chill in the pit of his stomach and looked down.

At some point, Linel had removed her short sword from its sheath and had buried the tip in Eugeo's stomach by about five cens.

It had only looked like a wooden toy before. The wood he'd taken to be the blade had actually been the scabbard. The blade she pulled from it was not made of wood but an unfamiliar metal that appeared cloudy green. The surface caught the outside light and gleamed wetly.

"Eu—!"

That was Kirito. He craned his neck to look back at his partner, frozen in place, right foot forward. Fizel had been at Linel's side just an instant earlier, but now she was standing behind Kirito, thrusting her own green blade into his black shirt. Just as before, her smile was triumphant and confident.

"And I am Fizel Synthesis Twenty-Nine."

They pulled their short swords from Eugeo and Kirito simultaneously. With swipes so fast they were invisible, Fizel and Linel flicked the blood off their blades and returned them to their sheaths.

The chill that snuck into his stomach began to spread to his whole body. Everywhere that freezing feeling touched, his sensations began to numb.

"You're...Int...eg...," he managed to stammer before even his tongue froze in his mouth. Eugeo felt his knees give way, and then he toppled to the floor. His chest and left cheek smashed against the marble, but he didn't even feel an impact, much less any pain.

A second later, he heard Kirito hit the floor, too.

Poison, he belatedly realized, trying to think of a counterplan.

In class at Swordcraft Academy, they had learned about poisons and antidotes found in the natural world. But all the cases presented were from sources like plants, snakes, and insects. The school never even considered the possibility that they would be attacked with poisons in battle.

But of course. At the school—in the entirety of the human realm—battle was merely a competition of ferocity and aesthetics. Spreading toxic substances on a weapon was completely against the rules. Even that noble boy who released a poisonous insect to impede their advancement at the Zakkaria tournament didn't actually put any on his blade in competition.

So the extent of Eugeo's knowledge of poisons was: If such and such bug stings you, rub such and such herb on it. He didn't know what kind of poison the girls used, and there wasn't a single natural object around, much less an antidote herb. The last resort would be to attempt cleansing via sacred arts, but that was impossible while his hands and mouth were paralyzed.

So if this poison was the kind that both immobilized them *and* steadily drained their life, they could easily perish before they reached even the halfway point of Central Cathedral.

"You don't have to be so frightened, Eugeo," said Linel Synthesis Twenty-Eight overhead. Her high-pitched voice was warped and warbled; the poison made everything sound like it was underwater. "It's just a paralysis poison. But the only difference is whether you die here or on the fiftieth floor."

She trotted over until a little brown shoe came into Eugeo's vision where he lay with his cheek pressed to the floor. Linel lifted her foot and rested the toe right on Eugeo's head, rolling it around in search of something.

"...Hmm, no horns after all."

The foot moved over to his back, where it pressed down repeatedly on either side of his spine.

"And no wings, either. What about him, Zel?"

"He's just plain human, too!"

Somewhere outside of his field of view, Fizel was doing the same thing to Kirito. She said, "Aww, just when I thought we'd finally get to see some Dark Territory monsters!"

"Don't worry. If we take them up to the fiftieth floor and chop off their heads in front of everyone standing around up there, they should finally give us our divine weapons and dragons. Then we can just fly to the Dark Territory and see the real monsters for ourselves."

"Good point. Okay, Nel, let's race to see who can take out a dark knight first!"

To Eugeo's mind, the most horrifying part of all of this was how Fizel and Linel still sounded as childlike and innocent as ever. Why were children like them turned into Integrity Knights—and why were there children inside Central Cathedral at all?

Eugeo hadn't seen Linel draw her sword, and she had been

right in front of him. Fizel was quick enough to easily neutralize Kirito from a distance. Their abilities were undeniable.

But true skill in battle had to be gained through years of training and experience in battles of life and death. Eugeo's ability to wield the divine Blue Rose Sword was not just because he had swung an ax at the Gigas Cedar for years, but it was also because of his battle against the goblins in the Northern Cave, according to Kirito.

Fizel and Linel, however, looking to be no more than ten years old, didn't act like they'd ever faced the monsters from the world's extremities in battle. So how had they developed this blinding speed and skill?

Eugeo could not give voice to any of these questions. The poison had spread throughout his entire body, such that he didn't feel the coldness of the floor or any sensation that suggested he had a body at all. Linel grabbed Eugeo's right ankle with a tiny hand and started dragging him along, which he only realized because his vision rotated.

By turning his eyeballs to the left—the only part of him he could apparently move—Eugeo saw that Fizel was tugging Kirito along like a piece of luggage. His partner's face was impossible to read, owing to the same paralysis.

The young Integrity Knights lightly skipped up the stairs, dragging the boys with their swords still in place. With each step, his head bounced violently, but he still felt no pain.

If there was any time to think of a way out, it was then, but the paralyzing poison seemed to work on his brain, too, as Eugeo's mind was empty and numb.

Even for a foe he had sworn to fight, Eugeo found it difficult to believe that the Axiom Church was performing its inhumane knighting ceremony on mere children. After all, the population of the world had believed that this organization represented absolute goodness and justice—for centuries.

"You find it strange, don't you?" he heard Linel say, a hint of mirth in her voice. "Why are these children Integrity Knights? Well, since we're about to kill you anyway, I can explain first."

"If we're going to kill them, Nel, talking is a waste of energy. You're such an eccentric."

"It's going to be a boring trip up to the fiftieth floor. You see, Eugeo, we were born and raised here in the cathedral. Administrator herself ordered the monks and nuns in the tower to create us—in order to test out a resurrection sacred art that can heal totally lost life."

Despite the horrific nature of what she was saying, Linel's voice was utterly pleasant. "The children outside earn their Calling when they turn ten, but we got ours at five. Our job was to kill each other. We got these little toylike swords, even smaller than our poison blades, and would take turns stabbing each other."

"You were *terrible* at it, Nel. It hurt and hurt, every single time," Fizel interjected.

"Only because you would jump around in weird ways," Linel complained. "As you two probably know, since you've already defeated multiple knights, humans are surprisingly hard to kill. Even at five years old. So we would stab and slice, trying to kill the other as quickly as possible, and when the life would finally go down to zero, Administrator would bring us back to life with her sacred arts..."

"And the resurrection barely even worked at all in the beginning. The ones who died normally had it best. The ones who were exploded into bits or lumped into blobs of flesh would practically come back as different people altogether."

"It might have been our Calling, but we didn't want to go to all the trouble of getting hurt and not come back to life. We did a bunch of research together about the cleanest and quickest way to kill, because that had the least pain and the highest rate of successful resurrection. The problem is what you do for that single blow itself. Do you stab the heart as quickly and smoothly as possible or lop off the head?"

"I think we were about seven when we were finally able to do that. We would do all our practice swings while the other kids were sleeping."

His bodily sensation showed no signs of returning yet, but Eugeo still imagined the prickling of his hair standing on end.

In other words, Fizel's and Linel's extraordinary physical capabilities were the result of years of practice killing each other. Each and every day, they focused on nothing but how best to end each other's lives.

He supposed that practice of this sort would indeed be enough to grant even a child the right to be an Integrity Knight. But at what cost? These children had entirely lost a crucial part of themselves that would never return.

The constant shuffle up the staircase continued, as did Linel's pleasant tone of voice. "Administrator gave up on the resurrection tests when we were about eight. It seems that total resurrection was impossible in the end. Did you know that when your life goes to zero, a bunch of arrows of light come down and they kind of, like, carve your mind down? The kids who lost important parts of themselves that way never went back to normal, even after resurrection. There were many times that I came back and couldn't remember what had happened in the last few days. There were thirty of us in total when the experiment started, and by the end, only Zel and I were left."

"Since we survived and the test was over," Fizel said, "those old senate fuddy-duddies said we had to choose our next Calling, and we told them we wanted to be Integrity Knights. They got mad and said that Integrity Knights were summoned from Heaven by Administrator, and kids like us couldn't be one of them. So we ended up having a fight against the newest knights at the time...What were their names, again?"

"Umm...it was Something Synthesis Twenty-Eight and Twenty-Nine."

"It's the *Something* I was asking for, Nel! Well, anyway, you should have seen the looks on those senators' faces when we lopped off those cocky guys' heads in one shot."

The girls giggled, and Linel continued the story. "...So Administrator made a special exception and named us Integrity Knights in the place of the two who died. But since we haven't learned enough to go on defensive duties like the other knights, we still have to spend a two-year period learning the laws and sacred arts like the other apprentices. It's really getting old."

"We were just wondering how to hurry up and get our dragons and Divine Object weapons, when an alert went out that agents of the Dark Territory were loose in the cathedral. So we decided this was our chance! If we caught them before the other knights and executed them, Administrator would surely make us full-fledged knights at last. That's why we were waiting on the stairs."

"Sorry about using that poison. But we really wanted to take you up to the fiftieth floor alive, if possible. Oh, and don't worry—we're really good at killing, so it won't hurt."

The girls could scarcely wait for the moment when they dropped the boys' severed heads before the Integrity Knights' defensive line on the fiftieth floor. They bounded up the stairs with surprising speed, dragging their heavy prey behind them.

Despite the increasingly urgent need to devise an escape plan, all Eugeo could do was listen passively to their story. Even if his mouth wasn't paralyzed, it seemed impossible that he could actually talk the girls out of it. They didn't even seem to possess the concepts of good and evil. The only thing they obeyed was the order of their creator, the pontifex Administrator.

After dozens of times changing direction, the ceiling that formed the entirety of what Eugeo could see went from being a steady upward slope to a flat surface like any ordinary ceiling. There was no more staircase to travel—they had arrived at the Great Hall on the fiftieth floor that marked the midpoint of the cathedral.

Fizel and Linel stopped walking and exchanged brief comments about getting ready.

There were maybe minutes left—seconds, perhaps—before that green blade severed his neck. No matter how hard he willed, he couldn't even budge a finger; there was no sensation in his body.

The ceiling here was taller than anywhere previous, probably a good twenty mels overhead. The curved marble featured brilliant portraits of the three goddesses of creation and their followers. The circular pillars supporting the ceiling were covered in a multitude of sculptures and reliefs. On either side of the hall were massive windows beaming in the light of Solus. It was a tremendous sight, a place worthy of the name "Great Hall of Ghostly Light."

The girls dragged Eugeo and Kirito five mels forward, then came to a stop. The momentum left Eugeo's body in a half-turn, giving him a full view of the Great Hall at last.

It was frighteningly vast, seemingly spanning the entire breadth of the cathedral floor for one chamber. The distant corners of the multicolored stone floor were hazy through the light. A deep-red carpet ran from the entrance all the way to the far wall, where double doors stood, so tall they seemed to be built for a giant. Clearly, the stairs to continue moving upward were through that door.

In the middle of the hall, far before the giant door, a number of knights stood in their armor and helmets, bristling and forbidding, preventing further progress. Four of them stood in an evenly spaced row, and another waited slightly ahead.

The four in the back all wore brilliant silver armor and helmets with a cross-shaped slit in the middle—exactly the kind that Eldrie wore. Their weapons were identical longswords, each standing on its tip with its owner's hands resting heavily on the pommel.

The knight in the front looked much different from the others. This one's armor shone with a regal pale-purple color and looked comparatively delicate, and a thin sword designed for thrusting hung at the knight's side. It was tempting to think of this as "light" armor, but the suffocating sense of danger rolling off the one wearing it far outclassed the others. The knight's face was hidden under a helmet designed to resemble a bird of prey's wings, but it was clear that he or she was just as mighty as Deusolbert.

Five Integrity Knights, an incredibly imposing wall to surpass in order to continue upward—and yet, at that moment, it was the two little girls right next to them who represented a greater threat to Eugeo's and Kirito's lives.

Linel and Fizel, standing proud in their apprentice habits, faced the five knights.

"You must be Fanatio Synthesis Two, the vice commander of the knights," Linel said crisply. "If Fanatio of the Heaven-Piercing Blade is being called upon, then the senate must be panicked indeed. Or are *you* the worried one, Fanatio? At this rate, you might find your vice seat taken by the Osmanthus, won't you?"

After several seconds of strained silence, the purple knight spoke. The metallic voice carried that familiar inhuman rattle unique to Integrity Knights, but Eugeo did not miss its note of irritation.

"...Why do you apprentice children barge onto the battlefield of honorable knights?"

"Oh, this is so stupid!" Fizel immediately shot back. "It's that insistence on honor and dignity that got two of the so-called invincible Integrity Knights beaten. But don't worry; we've caught the intruders, and we won't let any more harm come to the reputation of the knighthood!"

"We're about to chop off their heads, so watch closely and give the pontifex an accurate report. Not that I would expect an 'honorable knight' to claim the credit like a coward."

Despite the desperate circumstances, Eugeo couldn't help but be amazed at the boldness of Linel and Fizel and how they stayed so composed facing five superhuman warriors.

But, no...Perhaps he was wrong. The emotion exuding from their little figures—was that...hatred?

With all his strength, Eugeo focused his eyes on the girls. Even if his intuition was correct, *what* did they hate? They'd showed nothing but pure curiosity toward Eugeo and Kirito, who were high traitors to Administrator and the Axiom Church.

Linel and Fizel were so busy staring at the Integrity Knights with open loathing and disrespect, the knights themselves were so obviously annoyed by them, and Eugeo was so preoccupied with trying to figure out the two girls, that it was unlikely *anyone* noticed the figure in black moving behind them until it actually appeared.

Like a panther on the hunt, despite suffering the same paralyzing toxin that Eugeo did, Kirito snuck behind the girls and grabbed their short swords from their belts, one with each hand. In one smooth movement, he drew the blades and pressed them against their exposed arms.

By the time they turned around, mouths agape, Kirito had already leaped clear backward, short swords in hand.

They were stunned. "Why...?"

"I can't move..."

The paralysis worked instantly, and after just a few words, the children toppled lightly to the floor. As they fell, Kirito rose. He held both poison daggers in one hand and stepped forward to search in their pockets with the other. In no time, he had found a little bottle the size of a fingertip, filled with an orange liquid.

He popped the cork out, sniffed it, and looked satisfied. Still paralyzed, Eugeo had no other option but to trust that it was an antidote as the bottle's contents slipped between his lips. It was probably for the best that his numb tongue couldn't taste it, either.

Kirito leaned down on his knee, an unfamiliar and severe look on his face, and whispered, "The paralysis will wear off in a few minutes. Once your lips work again, start chanting the Perfect Weapon Control command so the knights don't hear you. When it's ready, hang on to it and wait for my signal."

With that, he stood up and moved back to stand next to the girls. In a loud, clear voice, he called out to the five Integrity Knights, "The swordsmen Kirito and Eugeo apologize for the disrespect of entering your presence on our backsides! We seek to make amends and repair our dishonored reputations, and to cross swords with you!"

Promptly, the purple knight, who seemed to be the most important, replied, "I am second of the Integrity Knights, Fanatio Synthesis Two! Sinner, know that my divine Heaven-Piercing Blade knows not the concept of mercy, so if you wish to speak, do so while it remains sheathed!"

Kirito looked down at the collapsed girls next to him and, loud enough for the other knights to hear, said, "You must be wondering how I was able to move."

Linel was unable to speak, of course, but her eyes seemed to well up with frustration.

"You gave the game away. You said that all the monks and nuns were ordered to stay in their rooms. Nobody in the cathedral would dare disobey an order—so given that you weren't following them, you couldn't be real sisters-in-training."

The antidote started working, sending little prickles of pain into Eugeo's limbs, but he hardly noticed them at all. At last, he realized the nature of the emotion he saw on his partner's face.

Kirito—placid, aloof Kirito—was *furious*.

But his anger didn't seem to be directed at the children themselves. If anything, there was pain in his eyes when he glanced down at Linel and Fizel.

"And those sheaths you wear. They're made of ruby oak from the south. That's the only material that won't corrode when touched by these swords made of Ruberyl's poisoned steel. There's no way a simple apprentice nun would be carrying something like that. So before you approached, I cast a poison-dissolving art—it just took a little time for it to actually work. The speed of your sword isn't all there is to strength. In short, you were stupid enough that you might as well die here."

He held the poison swords aloft in his left hand, then swung them down without mercy or hesitation.

The two short swords flew, leaving little green trails. They thudded dully, the blades stuck into the floor right before Linel's and Fizel's noses.

"But I will not kill you. Instead, I want you to watch the Integrity Knights that you insulted and see how powerful they truly are."

Then he turned and took several steps forward. He drew his black sword loudly and swung around to brandish it before a knight.

"You have waited long enough, Fanatio! I challenge you!"

No…he wouldn't.

But Eugeo's lips could do no more than tremble. He couldn't call Kirito back; his mouth and tongue were still regaining their sensations.

Kirito often liked to take out books on weapons from the academy library, so that might explain how he knew about things like ruby oak and poisoned steel. It was just like him to employ his skills of observation to escape from the girls' trap, but the two had still undoubtedly left them in a far more dangerous situation than before. They had to face five Integrity Knights, one of whom was the vice commander, and fight them in direct battle. Their great idea about having Perfect Control ready to go before they entered the Great Hall was totally ruined.

Normally, Kirito would drag Eugeo away from this situation to regroup and improve their chances. That he wasn't doing it now was a sign that he wasn't in his right mind. He was gripped by such a rage that if Eugeo squinted, he thought he could see wisps of pale-blue flame rising from the back of his black shirt.

Even the instructors at Swordcraft Academy would be taken aback if they faced Kirito in his present state. But the purple knight named Fanatio, vice commander of all Integrity Knights, boldly grabbed the handle of his rapier and drew it. Eugeo's eyes were pierced with such a brilliant light that it seemed the weapon itself was glowing.

Following Fanatio, the other four soldiers flipped up their downward-pointed swords in unison and took stances. The swell of tension and hostility pushed back against Kirito's, making the air in the hall practically crackle.

Fanatio showed no signs of being affected by the tense mood. His dark voice issued forth from the helmet.

"Sinner Kirito, it seems that you desire a duel of single combat with me. Unfortunately, we are under strict orders to slaughter by any means necessary if you should reach the Great Hall. So you will fight *them* first—my personal students, the Four Whirling Blades!"

With that grand pronouncement, Fanatio promptly launched a System Call and began a complex, high-speed casting chant. It was most likely—most *definitely*—Perfect Weapon Control. They either had to use the same art to counteract it or attack before the spell was finished.

Kirito chose the latter. He sprang forward at Fanatio so hard that the hobnails on his boots created sparks. His black sword swung up high in the air.

But at the same moment, the leftmost of the four knights standing behind Fanatio began a similar charge. This one met Kirito with a two-handed greatsword, whipping it horizontally from the left.

Kirito changed the angle of his swing, bringing it straight down to block the knight's attack. There was an ear-rending screech of metal, and both combatants sprang backward, creating a gap between them.

Unlike the knight, who had to redirect the momentum of his massive sword, Kirito recovered quickly. By the time he landed, he was already in follow-up mode, ready to plunge in again and deliver one fatal blow—

"…?!"

Eugeo gasped. Somehow there was a second knight there, unleashing a devastating slice from Kirito's left. Kirito paused, tilting his sword up to slice left and deflect. There was another screech, a shower of sparks, and they ended up about four mels apart.

This second knight also ended up significantly off-balance. This was natural, as anyone swinging such a huge sword so hard would find it difficult to avoid the shift in momentum when it was knocked off its trajectory. If anything was worthy of praise here, it was Kirito's skill in repelling the enemy's attack with a minimum of movement, absorbing the impact, and promptly transitioning to the next move.

However—before Eugeo could even suspect it, the third knight was leaping at Kirito where he landed. Eugeo tore his eyes away from the third clash of blades and forced himself to look farther behind them.

"——!!"

His jaws clenched. By the time Kirito and the third knight's swords met, the fourth was already charging.

How could they predict his movements so accurately? Yet another sideways swipe, and this time, Kirito's reaction was off. He managed to block the swing, but the momentum finally pushed him back, and his black form teetered in the air.

That's it...

Belatedly, Eugeo realized the knights' intentions. All their attacks were horizontal swings from left to right. If he deflected them with his sword, that limited the direction he would be pushed. Then the next knight would rush to that spot and start another horizontal slash. Given the increased effective area of their attacks as compared to vertical slices or thrusts, and the size and length of their swords, it must have been easy enough for them to ensure that even when jumping early, they had enough leeway to hit Kirito no matter where he landed.

The Integrity Knights didn't have consecutive techniques the way the two boys did, but this was effectively the same thing, just spread out over a group. These were not the preening, demonstrative swordsmen of Centoria but true fighters with experience in the Dark Territory.

But even the Integrity Knights' combination strategy was not infallible.

Figure it out, Kirito! Then you can counteract it!

The only sound that erupted from Eugeo's throat was a dry groan. At least his tongue and lips were starting to move again. He worked at the tense muscles as best he could so that he'd be able to start his chant and silently prayed. *Figure it out, Kirito.*

After deflecting the fourth knight's attack, Kirito finally faltered on the landing and had to put a hand to the floor.

The first knight had recovered and blazed forward with another ferocious attack. Kirito promptly leaned backward, trying to duck under the sword. A lock of his black hair made contact with the blade and flew free.

Exactly. If he knew they were always going to swing horizontally, he could dodge above or below, rather than stopping it with his sword.

But that evasion had to be one with his countermove. If all he did was fall over to dodge, he would be that much slower to transition to his next action, if not worse.

And the second knight, who bore down on Kirito from the left, was not going to give him time to recover. He raised his sword from flat to overhead and started a massive downward swing.

"Ah…!"

Eugeo tried to yell *Watch out*, ignoring the sharp pain that stabbed at his throat. But he wasn't in time. Sensing that there would be no way to avoid it, his eyes instinctively tried to avert themselves from the grisly outcome.

Just then, the first knight, who had finished his swing to Kirito's right, suddenly lurched. Kirito hadn't just been lying on the ground. Somehow, he wrapped both his legs around one of the knight's and pulled the larger man down on top of him.

The second knight was already into his attack and couldn't stop now, so the huge greatsword dug deep into his companion's back. He tried to pull it away, visibly startled, when a dark blur rushed up from below.

Kirito thrust through the knight's upper arm as he jumped to his feet, then turned to the third knight, who was hastily trying to follow up, and hurled the second knight at him. The newer attacker had no choice but to stop before he simply sliced his partner in two.

At last, the combination attack of the group Fanatio called the Four Whirling Blades came to a halt.

Kirito took advantage of this brief interval to burst forward. He completely ignored the fourth knight and charged at Fanatio, who was still chanting his Perfect Weapon Control.

Make it in time! Eugeo prayed.

"Enhance—!" Fanatio shouted.

"Yaaaah!!" Kirito bellowed.

He swung back his sword, still at a considerable distance. Normally it would never reach from this far, but the blade promptly let off a pale-green light—the Aincrad-style attack Sonic Leap. Like Vertical, it was a single downward slice, but this one had a charging power that covered over twice the distance in an instant.

Kirito leaped like some hunting animal, trailing colored light, as Fanatio held out the tip of his rapier. But no matter what he did with it, such a slender tool could not completely block the impact of an ultimate technique. The Gigas Cedar blade was even heavier than Eugeo's divine Blue Rose Sword. When combined with the tremendous speed of Kirito's attack, *three* of those little rapiers together would shatter easily under its force.

The black swordsman reached the peak of his jump, and just as he started to swing the sword forward, the rapier *glinted* in the knight's hands. Or more accurately, the entire body of it flashed, and then it stretched forward at incredible speed.

The slender beam silently punctured Kirito's left flank, continued onward through the air, then exploded at last against the ceiling of the Great Hall. All of this happened in a single moment.

The shock of his pierced stomach threw off the trajectory of Kirito's attack, causing the brunt of its force to hit nothing but air and merely glance off the plume of Fanatio's helmet.

There was hardly any bleeding from the wound, so it didn't seem like much of a danger in terms of his life value, but Kirito immediately fell to a knee as he landed. Eugeo looked closer and saw that there was a faint trail of smoke rising from the edges of a little hole in his shirt.

So it was likely a fire-based attack. Yet the light that shot from Fanatio's sword was so white, it was nearly blue. Eugeo had never seen fire that color before.

Fanatio turned with almost detestable grace and pointed the tip of the rapier at the prone Kirito. It let off a soft hiss, and another beam of light shot out. If Kirito hadn't immediately leaped to his left, it would have caught his leg. Instead, the beam pierced into the marble floor and exploded again. When the light faded, there was a melted red hole in the spot.

"No...way...," Eugeo grunted, though he didn't even realize he'd done it at first.

The materials used to build the cathedral were the same excellent marble as the Everlasting Walls that divided Centoria, judging by the pure color and smooth sheen. It wasn't the kind of stone that would melt from a simple fire. Even Deusolbert's Conflagration Bow only succeeded in burning the carpets and tapestries.

So if Fanatio's Perfect Control arts were fire-based, they were easily far greater than Deusolbert's. It was possible that Kirito's life was already in dire condition from the earlier shot.

Clutched in the grips of cold fear, Eugeo could only watch as Kirito continued to leap around irregularly. Fanatio's sword flashed and blasted after him, gouging stone with each volley.

The most frightening part of the technique was that it operated instantly, with no preparatory period of charging or thrusting. From Eugeo's location, it was impossible to tell when the casually pointed rapier would emit the beam of light. It was similar to Eldrie's Frostscale Whip in terms of its range, but that one seemed positively cute compared to this.

Fanatio continued pressuring Kirito, gliding after him. It was only Kirito's honed primal instincts and excellent reflexes that helped him evade the fourth, fifth, and sixth beams.

It was the seventh that finally brought an end to the deadly game of cat and mouse.

The beam sizzled through the air and caught Kirito on the top of his right foot in midair. He lost balance and fell hard on his shoulder. Even then, he lifted himself up immediately, but Fanatio was there, training the point of his weapon below that black head of hair.

"Ki…!" Eugeo started to shout, but then he realized the numbness in his throat and mouth was finally subsiding for good. He thought he might have enough voice to execute the sacred art.

He summoned strength into his gut and began to recite the commands, quietly enough that the knights couldn't hear but loud enough for God.

"System Call…"

Kirito would be able to get out of his predicament on his own. There was only one thing for Eugeo to do, and that was to recite his Perfect Weapon Control and have it ready to go when it was needed.

Fanatio held his deadly sword directly before Kirito, drawing out the silence, and then muttered, "…For a hundred years, the commander has scolded me for a bad habit of taunting in these situations…but I must admit, it is so pathetic. Why do those who fall before the might of my Heaven-Piercing Blade always look so foolish? I am certain that you, too, are wondering about the nature of this attack that defeated you so easily."

The four knights working under Fanatio finished their healing, and they fanned out behind Kirito at a distance, brandishing their swords one-handed. That made escape more difficult, but it also looked like Fanatio's speech might last a while. Eugeo focused his entire mind on chanting, taking great pains not to make a single mistake.

"Sinner though you may be, if you lived in Centoria, then you must know what a mirror is," Fanatio prompted Kirito, who looked baffled by this sudden leap, despite his obvious agony.

A mirror?

Eugeo had seen them before, of course. Not back home in Rulid, but the rooms in the elite disciple dorm at the academy each had a small one. It was a curious item that reflected light far more vividly than water or metal plates, but Eugeo hadn't spent much time looking in it. He didn't like his weak-willed appearance.

Fanatio kept the sword trained on Kirito in case he moved, and continued, "It is an expensive item made by pouring molten silver into a case of glass, so few outside of Centoria will have seen one. A mirror can reflect the light of Solus with nearly perfect results. Do you understand me? Any place that receives both Solus's light and a reflected beam from a mirror is made twice as warm. One hundred and thirty years prior, our exalted pontifex summoned all the silver coins and crafts in Centoria, then ordered the glassmakers to fashion one thousand great mirrors from them. It was an experiment in creating a weapon that did not require a sacred arts chant to execute. A thousand mirrors, arranged in a semicircle in the cathedral's courtyard, could focus all of Solus's midsummer strength into one point and produce pure-white flame. Within minutes, it could melt down a rock the size of a person."

Weapon... White flame...?

Fanatio's statement didn't exactly add up in Eugeo's mind. But he could sense instinctively that this plan of the pontifex's was just as horrific as making children kill each other in order to test resurrection arts.

"Ultimately, the pontifex decided it was too elaborate to utilize in battle. But she did not want all the work to go to waste, and so she had those thousand mirrors bundled and strengthened and honed down into a single sword: the Heaven-Piercing Blade. Do you understand me, sinner? It was the power of Solus itself that pierced your stomach and foot!"

Eugeo was so stunned by this proud speech, he nearly slipped up at the end of the chant.

So the white beam of light was Solus, amplified by the power of a thousand mirrors.

An attack with heat elements could be fought off with ice elements. But how would one defend against an attack of pure light? And as far as Eugeo knew, no art that used light elements as its base had any direct attack power to speak of. An illusory light spell could be eliminated by one using darkness, but not even ten or twenty layers of darkness could withstand a beam of that power.

Eugeo continued with his recitation largely automatically, resisting the sense of panic driving him, and finally reached the end. All he had to do was finish with *Enhance Armament*, and the Blue Rose Sword would unleash its hidden strength. Now he had to wait for Kirito's signal.

Fanatio had said all he wanted to say and pushed forward the rapier he had pointed at Kirito's head.

"Kirito, do you understand now the full power of the sword that will take your remaining life? Before you die, repent for your sins, pledge your faith to the three goddesses, and beg for forgiveness. Then the purity of the ghostly light will wash your sins clean and guide your soul to Heaven. And now I bid you farewell, young, foolish heretic."

The Heaven-Piercing Blade flashed, surging with the beam of light that would pierce Kirito's heart and end his life.

At that exact same moment, Eugeo heard, "Discharge!"

Before the light erupted from the tip of Fanatio's sword, Kirito smacked his hands together and shoved them forward. Right in front of his palms was a silver-colored sheet.

But it wasn't just an ordinary metal plate. It was perfectly square and flat, and in it, Eugeo could see a reflection of Fanatio's helmet.

Just before Kirito had brought his hands together, Eugeo had glimpsed two different-colored elements gripped in his fingers. In his right hand was a steel element, used to throw needles or create temporary tools. And in his left hand was a crystal element, an essence of glass for fashioning cups or building barriers that were hard to see. By combining the two and forming them into a flat surface, he had created…

…a mirror.

The spear of superheated light hit the magically created mirror and instantly turned the silver into orange.

Tools created from sacred elements were naturally short-lived. It might look like the same knife, but one forged from proper ore would last for decades, while a tool crafted from steel elements would run out of life and turn to dust in mere hours. This mirror was no exception, and it clearly wouldn't last against the Heaven-Piercing Blade's incredible power.

Sure enough, the mirror only held up for a tenth of a second. The liquefied mixture of glass and metal sprayed outward, and 80 percent of the beam's power proceeded toward Kirito.

He made use of that instant, however. By tilting his body to the left *just* enough, it singed his hair and a bit of his cheek as it passed him.

The other 20 percent of the beam reflected by the mirror bounced sharply back at Fanatio's helmet.

Despite the stunning turnaround, the second of all Integrity Knights yanked his head aside with similarly quick reflexes. But the winglike plumes on either side of the helmet did not escape damage. The light penetrated the left wing, obliterated the fastener that held it down—and then the entire helmet fell off in two halves, front and back.

The first thing Eugeo noticed was the volume of hair that burst free.

It was just as black as Kirito's, yet the shine of it was far richer. The long, wavy locks, which must have required a lot of upkeep, shone in the midday sun from the Great Hall's window.

Wow, for being a knight, he's kinda…, Eugeo started to think, and then Fanatio raised a hand to block the light and shouted, "You dare see me, you knave?!"

Unlike the metallic, warped voice that came from the helmet, this one was clear and high-pitched.

It's a woman?!

In his shock, Eugeo nearly discarded the sacred arts he had in

waiting. He clamped his lips shut and tried to focus on holding the spell in. But part of him couldn't avoid staring at Fanatio's back.

She was as tall as Kirito, if not taller, but seen in this new light, the curve from back to waist was indeed too delicate. And yet he had never doubted that Fanatio was a man until that point.

They'd already met Alice Synthesis Thirty and the children Linel and Fizel, so there was no reason to assume there weren't plenty of women among the Integrity Knights. And at the academy, nearly half the students were girls like Ronie and Tiese. Many of those students wound up to be Integrity Knights, so it shouldn't have been a surprise that the second-in-command was a woman.

Eugeo was puzzled by why he was so thrown for a loop, until he realized that Fanatio's mannerisms and attitude were extremely masculine. So perhaps Fanatio's current rage wasn't about the revelation of her face—but her femininity.

Even Kirito looked completely shocked, one knee on the ground and burns on his face.

Fanatio glared at him through the fingers of her left hand and said, "And you...you look at me the same way, sinner? Even a traitor and rebel against the Church claims that he cannot fight me seriously once he knows I am a woman?"

Despite her strangled cry, her voice was as pure and beautiful as an instrument played by a master musician.

"I am not human. I am an Integrity Knight summoned to earth from Heaven...and yet you men mock and slander me as soon as you learn I am a woman! And not just my fellows...but even the general of the dark knights, the very manifestation of evil!!"

No, you're wrong. Neither I nor Kirito is mocking you, Eugeo thought.

Between the garrison at Zakkaria and the academy, he had fought against many women. Many were better than he was and had bested him in combat. In none of those battles did Eugeo fight at less than his best because they were women, and he held an equal regard for the skilled, no matter their sex.

Sword Art Online: Alicization Rising 12

But what if it wasn't a fight with rules for victory and defeat, but a true battle to the death? Could he actually destroy the last of an opponent's life without hesitation?

The breath caught in Eugeo's throat. He'd never had to consider this question.

Just then, Kirito launched himself up into the air. It wasn't a fancy technique of any kind, just a slash from the upper right. It was so fast that Eugeo could barely see the blade moving. It was practically a miracle that Fanatio was able to block it in time, given her distress. An earsplitting clang ripped through the vicinity, sparks briefly illuminating the faces of the two combatants.

Fanatio caught the sword on the rapier's guard, but the momentum of the attack drove her several steps back. Kirito did not let up any pressure on the knight as they clashed hilt to hilt. Bit by bit, Fanatio's purple-armored knee began to bend.

Voice low, Kirito said, "I see. That's why you chose that sword and that move. So that you could fire those shots and keep anyone from finding out you were a woman...Isn't that right, Miss Fanatio?"

"You...y-you wretch!!" she shrieked, pushing back on her sword.

At great pains, Eugeo tore his eyes away from the combatants to look at the four knights surrounding them, who did seem slightly unnerved. Perhaps even some of *them* were unaware of Fanatio's true identity. He had no idea about the two paralyzed girls to his right, though.

Kirito and Fanatio continued their deadlock, soaking in the attention of all present. In terms of personal and sword weight, Kirito had a clear advantage. But once she pushed back on equal footing, Fanatio exhibited a tremendous force of her own that did not seem to come from her physical arms.

Through gritted teeth, Kirito tried rattling her again. "...Just so you know, the reason I was so shocked earlier is because your spirit got so weak as soon as the helmet broke. You hide your face and your swordfighting style...I'd say you're the one who's most obsessed with your femininity."

"Sh-shut up! I'll kill you...I swear I'll kill you!"

"That's the point of this fight. And I'm certainly not going to let up just because you're a woman. I've lost to girls plenty of times already!"

Even from just what Eugeo knew, Kirito had lost to Sortiliena, his tutor disciple at school, plenty of times. But the way he was speaking now, it didn't sound like he was talking about training and practice duels. It sounded like he had engaged in real, actual battles against swordswomen and lost...

Kirito abruptly swung his right foot forward and swept her leg. Her balance lurched, and the two blades gave off sparks. He pushed the jet-black sword forward with one hand.

But the Integrity Knight flashed her hand with impossible speed, and the rapier deflected the side of the black sword like a living creature. With his thrust pushed aside, she had time to recover her balance and take a step back for distance.

Kirito countered just as quickly. He plunged in close, practically ramming her, to keep the gap small. Given the way she could produce that light beam without any preparation, fighting at a distance was a nonstarter.

A swordfight erupted at point-blank range and lightning speed.

Most shocking of all to Eugeo was that for all of Kirito's blinding combination attacks, Fanatio met every one without faltering. Her shining rapier moved here and there and everywhere, dispatching every strike of the black blade that just kept coming. Whenever the slightest opening presented itself, she threw in two or three jabs in a row. Neither was using any ultimate techniques, because neither had the time to take the proper stance.

None of the sword schools in the human realm possessed anything like the combination attacks of the Aincrad style. Even the veteran Integrity Knight Deusolbert wasn't aware of them. That would mean that Fanatio's combos were something she came up with herself. Surely, the reason for that had something to do with what Kirito had said earlier.

The Heaven-Piercing Blade defeated foes without letting them approach. The combination attacks ensured that if she couldn't use Perfect Weapon Control, she could continue attacking, even if the first blow was blocked.

Fanatio was terrified of fighting at ultraclose range and having what was underneath her armor revealed.

But why…? Why would she go to such lengths to hide her own nature?

Eugeo watched their battle in stunned rapture as he considered these questions. The other four knights were in the same state of mind—they were all watching with their greatswords lowered.

Wow…

What a truly brilliant battle.

Even at such close range, both combatants kept their feet still and traded furious storms of slashes and thrusts, dodging and deflecting as necessary. It felt like he was watching shooting stars clash, reflecting and vanishing. The impact of steel on steel was so quick and constant that it began to resemble a kind of percussion performance.

A ferocious smile was plastered on Kirito's pale, excited face as he moved, a single being of man and sword. The strategy was to stick close to prevent her from using the Solus attack, but at this point, he just seemed to be enjoying unleashing his swordfighting skill.

But Fanatio had no need to indulge him. She could have one of her knights attack Kirito from behind, then pull back and use her beams. He would have no defense against that.

Yet the Integrity Knight with the long black hair seemed to be determined to beat him at his own game. Eugeo couldn't guess what her reasons were. Was it anger at Kirito's taunts? Because her pride wouldn't allow her to back away? Or did she, too, find some value in trading combination attacks at the very limits of possibility?

Eugeo couldn't see Fanatio's face from his position, so he didn't know what kind of expression she was wearing. Based on what had been said, Fanatio seemed to have been an Integrity Knight serving the Church for at least 130 years, if not longer. It was an amount of time that Eugeo, who was not yet nineteen years old, could scarcely fathom.

So he had no way of knowing how many years ago she started hiding her face and gender, but if she had developed these combinations skills all on her own, it had to be over ten or twenty years. The only reason Kirito could keep up with Fanatio was that he was an expert practitioner of the rare Aincrad style. Any other swordsman would have been crushed flat without getting in a single swipe.

So perhaps Kirito was actually the first opponent Fanatio had ever been able to exhibit her utmost abilities against.

Based on the examples of Eldrie and Deusolbert, even the Integrity Knights prized the beauty and gallantry of the single attack. It was hard to imagine that Fanatio could utilize her combination skills in training against the other knights. For a long, long time, she had trained in secret against the imaginary shadow of another wielder of these arts—a shadow that now had flesh and blood in the person of Kirito.

As their superhuman duel continued, Eugeo eventually realized that all the hair on his body was standing on end, and his eyes were brimming with tears.

Ever since he started learning the Aincrad style with Kirito, he had been envisioning an ultimate form of battle that was now realized before him. This was not the practiced beauty of the principled aesthetic but the stark allure that could only result from the ultimate fixation on cutting down the enemy, and nothing else.

Five consecutive thrusts from Fanatio met five consecutive slashes from Kirito, and with each rebound they brought their weapons back around with even greater fury.

"Ryaaaa!"

"Seyaaaa!"

The shock waves of their weapons intersecting felt hot on Eugeo's skin, even from where he lay on the floor a considerable distance away. Their black hair danced and flew, metal snarled, and they switched spots, back and forth.

When Fanatio's face finally came into view, Eugeo's breath caught in his throat.

She had the pure beauty of a holy woman from fairy tales come to life. By appearance, she couldn't have been more than in her mid-twenties, with smooth skin the color of tea mixed with plenty of milk. Her arched brows and long lashes were black, but her irises were a light brown very close to gold. She appeared to come from the eastern region, with a slender-bridged nose and a rounded chin that added softness to her beauty. Her small lips had just the faintest tinge of red.

There was none of the lethal fury in her features that he'd felt earlier. Instead, there was simply determination, enclosing and protecting a kind of pain.

"Ah, I see," said Fanatio in her smooth voice as their swords crossed. "Sinner, you are not like the others I have fought until today. No man has ever looked upon this cursed visage and truly attempted to kill me."

"Cursed, huh? Then who are you combing your hair and wearing lipstick for?" Kirito taunted. But Fanatio merely grimaced.

"For over a hundred years, I have waited in hope that the man I love might seek something in me other than my skill with the sword and the number of heads I bring him. But after pining behind my mask for so long, and then tasting defeat at the hands of a newer knight more beautiful than me, who bothered not to hide her features...I could not help but seek a touch of cosmetics."

A knight more beautiful and mighty than Fanatio. A woman.

The thought of yet more powerful knights in the tower gave Eugeo the chills, but then he realized that he *knew* of an Integrity Knight who fit the description. A recent knight who did not wear a helmet, and who had dispatched him with a single blinding strike—Alice Synthesis Thirty.

Kirito must have felt something in her words, too, but he kept his face an utter mask as he demanded, "What is the most important thing to you? If all the Integrity Knights do is obey the pontifex's orders, then there shouldn't be any room in your heart for love or jealousy. I don't know who this man is, but if you've been in love with him for a hundred years...then it's because you're human. You're just as human as me. I'm fighting to destroy the Church and your leader so that human beings like you can fall in love and lead happy lives!"

Even Eugeo was stunned by this speech. Kirito was always so aloof; he had no idea his partner was thinking about such deep concepts. But Eugeo also sensed his friend was grappling with himself as well.

For just an instant, Fanatio's expression twisted.

When a deep furrow appeared on her smooth forehead, he wondered if her Piety Module would emerge the way Eldrie's did, but it was only the number-two Integrity Knight's extreme reaction.

"...Child, you have no idea what kind of hell this world will be plunged into without the might of the Axiom Church...Day by day, the Dark Territory amasses its forces. They bristle just beyond the boundary of the End Mountains. Yes, I admit that you are strong. And you are not an agent of darkness or a wicked intruder, contrary to what the prime senator claimed. But you are still dangerous. You threaten the Church and its knights not just with your sword but your words as well. In the face of our greatest duty, to protect the human realm and those who dwell in it, my feelings of love are but chaff in the dirt."

She looked stern and resolute, all reservations cast aside. All throughout her long speech, the Heaven-Piercing Blade and the black sword creaked and screamed at maximum volume. If either combatant pulled back even the tiniest amount, they would surely be thrown off balance.

Even as they struggled, the life of the two swords was dropping. If the deadlock continued, the Heaven-Piercing Blade would give out first. Among Divine Objects with similar rank, the larger and thicker weapon always had more life to begin with.

Naturally, Fanatio would be aware of this. She knew that if her sword gave out and left her open to attack, Kirito would slice her without mercy or hesitation.

"And that is why I must defeat you—even if it means trampling upon my pride as a knight. Mock me for winning with a shameful technique. You have that right," she muttered. Then she bellowed, "Hidden light of the Heaven-Piercing Blade, cast off your shackles!! Release Recollection!!"

That was it—the command to unleash its greatest power!

The silver blade shone brighter than it ever had.

An instant later...

Bwaash! A multitude of beams streamed outward from the tip of the weapon. *A blinding attack*, was Eugeo's first reaction. It was a way to rob Kirito of vision and throw him off balance so that she could strike.

But that possibility was ruled out when one of the beams in the omnidirectional spray landed on the stone floor right next to Eugeo and gouged deep into the marble.

That's no blinding technique—they're all *the same beams! Kirito!!* Eugeo thought desperately, sitting upright. Just at that moment, one of the beams was about to pierce Kirito's right arm. And in fact, there were charred black holes on his left shoulder and right thigh already.

Kirito wasn't the only one who was suffering from the superheated light.

Even Fanatio, the very owner of the Heaven-Piercing Blade, received ugly holes on the armor over her stomach, shoulders, and legs. The punctures looked even deeper than Kirito's. And yet there wasn't a single shred of anything but determination in her proud features.

The Integrity Knight Fanatio Synthesis Two was going to put a stop to Kirito, and she would sacrifice her life to do so.

Eugeo recalled what the previous pontifex, Cardinal, had said. The Release Recollection command summoned all of the weapon's memories and unleashed its wildest power. Power that was enough to destroy not just the enemy but the wielder as well.

The unleashed Heaven-Piercing Blade's initial volley inflicted nearly fatal wounds on the two directly in its presence, and it caused at least minor damage to the other four knights at a distance. The stately, impressive decorations in the Great Hall were hideously blasted and charred, and expensive glass windows shattered left and right. Few of the lights reached Eugeo or the two paralyzed girls beside him, but eventually they would get hit.

The lights shone and shone from the tip, but the weapon forged of a thousand mirrors showed no signs of stopping. Every second, the tip of the sword flashed, sending out short bursts of light in every direction. Half went up into the air, hitting the walls, pillars, and ceiling, but many of those that traveled downward naturally landed on the two people closest to the source.

Without letting up any pressure on the intersection of the swords, Kirito craned and darted his head out of the way of any beams threatening to hit his brow. More light-headed for Fanatio's face, but the Integrity Knight did not budge. A beam brushed her cheek, gouging a deep red furrow into her spotless skin and evaporating a lock of her full black hair.

"You...colossal idiot!!" Kirito screamed. A spray of blood shot from his mouth. No matter how much life Kirito had, there was no question about being in danger of running out, given the damage he was taking. But the swordsman in black refused to falter. He slid his sword up so the side of it covered the beam-emitting point of the Heaven-Piercing Blade.

Brief as this moment was, it succeeded in blocking all of the light that was shooting at Kirito and Fanatio.

Now—now is the moment!

Kirito did not give an explicit signal, but Eugeo's senses of reason and intuition both told him that the time had come.

Fanatio and her four knights, who held up their greatswords like shields, were too busy with the light beams to pay any attention to the other guilty party. No one was going to take advantage of the moment of weakness when Eugeo activated his Perfect Control.

He leaped up with tremendous force and drew the Blue Rose Sword he'd been cradling beneath his stomach the entire time.

"Enhance—"

In midair, he spun the handle so that it pointed down, added his left hand to the hilt, and thrust it into the marble floor with all his strength.

"—Armament!!"

Nearly half of the pale-blue blade sank into the stone.

Craaakk!! With an earsplitting bursting sound, the marble was instantly covered in white frost.

Sharp, crystalline pillars thrust upward in a wave of ice that swelled forth. Within five seconds of launching, the ten-mel-wide ice wave had swallowed up the feet of Kirito, Fanatio, and the four other knights.

At last, the quartet of knights noticed the anomaly. Their helmeted heads turned to look in his direction.

But it was too late.

Eugeo clenched the sword with all his strength and screamed, "Roses—*bloom*!!"

Instantly, countless vines of pale-blue ice sprang up around the feet of the knights, Fanatio, and Kirito. Each one was only the width of a pinkie finger, but every single tendril bristled with sharp thorns that dug into the legs of their prey.

"Rrgh…"

"Wh-what is this?!"

The knights exclaimed their surprise. By then, the icy vines were climbing up their legs and to their waists and bellies. One knight belatedly tried to sever the vines with his greatsword, but the moment the weapon touched the ice, more vines wrapped around it and sewed it to the ground.

The vines covered the knights from toes to fingertips to head, turning them into immobile ice sculptures. The ice creaked as it snaked upward, firming its grasp on its prey, and then, with the crisp ringing like a bell, it sprouted a multitude of dark-blue roses.

They were all ice, of course. There was no nectar or scent coming from the hard, crystalline buds, only freezing white mist. Soon the air in the hall was filled with it: a thick, sparkling haze. The source powering the chill was the very life of the captured knights.

The drain on their life was slow, but there was no way to summon the strength to break the chains of ice while the roses sucked it away. This sacred art was not designed for killing foes. Eugeo had settled on this particular effect for the purpose of immobilizing Alice.

The four knights were completely neutralized, but their worthy leader was sharp enough to intuit the nature of the attack as soon as the vines started breaking through the frost on the floor, and she jumped away to evade them.

But Kirito's reflexes were even quicker, aided by his prior understanding of Eugeo's technique. Improbably enough, he not only leaped earlier than Fanatio, but he landed on her shoulder armor to leap a second time farther away. He did a somersault in the air to distance himself from the vines of ice, spreading a fine spray of blood as he went.

The pressure of his jump pushed Fanatio back to the floor, where she landed on one knee and was immediately surrounded by the ice.

"Rrgh...!"

Her concentration faltered, and the indiscriminate shower of light beams from her sword succeeded in severing a few of the vines before it fell silent. Her hideously damaged purple armor was wreathed in fine tendrils, then covered in thick ice.

Blue roses sprouted up her body, the last one appearing right over the wound on her cheek. The penultimate Integrity Knight and her divine weapon stilled completely.

Kirito continued his backward leaps and flips to evade the ice vines, despite the terrible injuries all over his body. Eventually he lost his balance on a landing and fell right next to Eugeo.

"Grf..."

A little cough emerged from deep in his throat, spraying out an alarming amount of blood. It soon froze over into crimson frost, to Eugeo's alarm.

"Kirito...hang on, I'll use a healing art on you...!"

"No! Don't stop the technique!" Kirito demanded, eyes flashing despite the loss of color in his skin. "That isn't enough to stop her..."

Flecks of blood around his lips, he used the black sword as a crutch to hold his battered body upright. After wiping his mouth, closing his eyes, and getting his breath under control, Kirito glared and held his sword aloft.

"System...Call!!"

Given the state of his body, the speed of his desperate chanting was really remarkable. Between every command was a blood-curdling wheeze, and occasionally a bit of crimson spittle flecked from the corner of his lips. But still he continued to recite the dozen-plus commands of the art.

Up close, the sight of the numerous marks on Kirito's body was ghastly. The light from the Heaven-Piercing Blade had punctured him everywhere, and the wounds were charred and black. The only upside was that he hadn't lost much blood, but several of the beams had pierced his organs. His life was dropping faster than the knights trapped by the ice roses, and he needed help immediately.

But Eugeo couldn't let go of the hilt of his sword if he wanted to maintain his hold on the Perfect Control arts. Kirito might have been able to heal himself, but he was so viciously focused on his recitation that it was clear he had no such intention.

You don't need to rush, Kirito. Those knights won't break their cages of ice that quickly, Eugeo thought, looking up at the soldiers ahead.

Just then, a beam of light shot from the midst of the profusion of ice roses and stuck in the wall. He was so startled that he grunted, "Wha..."

The source of the light was Fanatio, who should have been completely immobilized under all those vines of ice.

Perfect Weapon Control wasn't some infinite power once the sacred art was cast. In order to control the expanded power of the weapon, the caster expended considerable concentration. Eugeo had to clutch the hilt of the sword stuck into the floor and continue envisioning the wild sprouting roses in order to maintain his prison of ice.

Fanatio had unleashed her sword's Perfect Control, fired sunrays, engaged in a light-speed battle with Kirito, then unleashed indiscriminate beams all over and suffered nearly fatal wounds for it. Her concentration should have been shot, and her control over the Heaven-Piercing Blade gone.

And yet...

The slender weapon covered in ice and clutched in Fanatio's right hand was slowly moving, creaking and crackling. Before Eugeo's stunned eyes, a wisp of steam, like the essence of her fighting spirit, rose from the knight's body.

"*Rrgh...!*"

He bit his lip and clutched the hilt of his sword even harder. Guided by this image, ten or so fresh vines of ice rose around Fanatio. They struck her right arm like whips and wrapped around it, forcing her to be still.

But that lasted for only a second. The knight shrugged off the clinging thorns of ice and forced her arm down. Nearly half of the azure vines shattered and spilled to the ground.

A chill colder than ice ran down Eugeo's back.

Is she even human?

Kirito was exhibiting tremendous force of will with his bloody recitation, but this woman was beyond even him. The uncontrollable light-beam attack had riddled her with holes, and the ice roses were mercilessly draining her life—and yet she still did not fall. Instead, she was ripping herself free from the chains of ice that her companion knights were helpless to stop, using nothing but the strength of one arm.

With horror, Eugeo noticed that the Heaven-Piercing Blade in her hand was steadily changing angle to point in their direction.

What was giving Fanatio so much strength?

Was it the Integrity Knight's sense of compelling duty to uphold the law? Her love for this man that had apparently lasted for a hundred years? Or did it have something to do with what she'd said earlier...?

Fanatio claimed that if the Axiom Church's power was lost, the armies of the Dark Territory would run wild over the human world.

If true, then she was sacrificing her own health for the sake of the common people—the ones the higher nobles treated like livestock, abusing and exploiting them for all they were worth.

But that couldn't be true. The Integrity Knights were the tools of the wicked Administrator, who took young Alice away, robbed her of her memories, and turned her into someone else. They were the hateful enemy. Their whole quest up the length of Central Cathedral had been built on the knowledge of their nature and the possibility that they would need to kill them.

They couldn't be anything else—the Integrity Knights couldn't be a bastion of goodness now.

"You...you people have no goodness!!" Eugeo growled, pouring all the hostility welled up in his heart into the Blue Rose Sword.

Once again, a wave of ice vines grew around Fanatio, winding up her right arm and digging into her flesh with their thorns.

"Stop...just *stop*!!"

But although his heart was full of overwhelming hatred,

something spilled from Eugeo's eyes. He could not accept that they were tears; he refused to recognize that he was being moved by the sight of her foolish insistence on extending her own arm, despite the binding thorns that embodied Eugeo's hatred and fury.

The Integrity Knight's arm was tattered. A carpet of broken thorns stuck in her skin, her blood oozing out and freezing into hanging red icicles.

But it never stopped moving, lowering until the upright Heaven-Piercing Blade was pointed level, its tip directed right at Eugeo and Kirito.

Through the blur of tears, Eugeo saw the silver weapon shine brighter than ever before. The light was so bright that Fanatio must have been burning off the entire remainder of her life. He had to squint his wet eyes to shut it out; the light was as bright as if Solus itself had descended on the Great Hall.

I can't win. I just can't beat her. Eugeo sighed softly, watching the ice roses melt and break down from nothing more than exposure to her light.

But he wasn't going to simply close his eyes and wait for that sun to bring him death. He refused to give in to Fanatio's "righteousness" like that.

He would at least create one last rose in a symbol of spite. He summoned the last dregs of hatred from the depths of his heart for that final act of defiance—when Kirito finished his recitation and murmured, "You can't beat her with hatred, Eugeo."

"Huh…?"

Eugeo turned back and saw his partner with blood-flecked lips turned into a tense smile. "You didn't come all this way because you hate the Integrity Knights, right? It's because you want to get Alice back, to see her again…You're here because you love Alice. And your feelings aren't in any way inferior to her justice. Same for me…I want to protect the people of this world: you, Alice, even her. So we can't afford to give up and lose now…Right, Eugeo?"

Despite the desperate circumstances, Kirito's voice was calm.

The mysterious black swordsman smiled, nodded, and looked forward.

Just then, the Heaven-Piercing Blade unleashed its biggest and final flash.

It was a spear of light that not even all the beams until now, bundled together into one, could have matched. The light of the heavens, which Solus herself flung to banish the god of darkness—Vecta—in the age of creation, bore down as it prepared to burn everything in its path.

Kirito's eyes were wide with astonishing willpower. The final line of the chant left his mouth, a single note of defiance amid desperate odds.

"Enhance Armament!!"

The black sword, pointed straight ahead, pulsed.

From every surface, every angle, darkness poured forth.

A surge of pure, light-sucking black writhed, soared, and tangled. It, too, coalesced into a massive spear, thick enough to require both hands to encircle, and shot forward. The tip of the spear seemed to have physical form: a hard, sharp tip like obsidian. Eugeo recognized that texture—it was the wood of the giant tree he had spent every day of his youth chopping at, until just over two years ago. The prior form of the black sword: the Gigas Cedar.

In that moment of recognition, Eugeo understood the nature of the Perfect Weapon Control that Kirito had activated.

By awakening the dormant memories in the black sword, he had brought the proud giant tree, which resisted any effort to cut it down for centuries, back to life in this place. It wasn't the same size and shape, but it was certainly the same material.

Hardness, sharpness, and overwhelming weight.

All three in such measure that its existence itself made it the largest weapon possible.

Eugeo felt his heart lurch. And then the tip of that void-dark spear made contact with the end of Solus's light. The resulting shock wave ripped through the Great Hall of Ghostly Light...and possibly rattled all of Central Cathedral itself.

The tremendous outpouring of heat and dense light did push back even the demon tree, bringing its relentless onslaught to a halt. Yet the endless darkness continued pouring out of the sword in Kirito's hands, propelling the weapon onward.

The Heaven-Piercing Blade showed no signs of stopping, either. The wild stream of light strengthened by the moment, until the heat had totally melted all of the ice roses keeping the knight captive. Not only that, but the gauntlet protecting her right arm was bright red and smoking.

Yet the stalemate between light and darkness in the center of the Great Hall continued.

But this sort of ultrapowerful clash could not possibly equal out and vanish into nothing. One sword would vanquish the other and utterly destroy its wielder.

And the one disadvantaged here was Kirito.

No matter how tough the Gigas Cedar was, it was a tree with physical form. Just as the real thing was eventually felled after years of chopping, it would take damage and gradually weaken until it was no more.

But the light of the Heaven-Piercing Blade was pure heat. How would one destroy a force without mass?

If there was a way to counteract that, it would have to be either a mirror, like Kirito had already tried, or some kind of absolute cold from the Blue Rose Sword—some special quality that was anathema to the light itself. But if the Gigas Cedar had any qualities, it was being incredibly hard and heavy...

And one other thing.

It greedily absorbed all of Solus's light and turned it into its own power.

Suddenly, Fanatio's spear of light splintered into a thousand tiny streams. It was Kirito's tree of darkness that broke the stalemate and resumed its charge.

The tip of his spear was, unsurprisingly, glowing red-hot, but it stood strong as it gouged through the sheer pressure of the light and bore down on its source. Meanwhile, the light itself sprayed wildly and landed all over the Great Hall, melting the ice vines and causing little explosions everywhere. The four other knights were blasted free from the ground and flew through the air.

Fanatio the Integrity Knight did not budge a step when she saw the enormous black lance approaching. Her beautiful features no longer contained any anger or hatred. Her eyelids fluttered down, and her lips budged. Surely there was some emotion contained in that action, but Eugeo could not detect what it was.

The sharp tip of the tree made its way up the stream to the source of the light at last, colliding with the end of the Heaven-Piercing Blade.

First, the silver rapier bent, then it twanged and rotated as it flew through the air. Then the knight herself launched backward with astonishing force. Her body flew directly toward the ceiling, spraying shards of purple metal and obliterating the painting of creation on the plaster.

Her fall was much slower. She came down with a shower of little pieces of structural marble and landed limply in front of the doors at the far end of the hall. The second Integrity Knight did not get up after that.

The spear of darkness gradually lost form and retreated like a shadow, retracting back into Kirito's sword. The blade itself seemed slightly bigger than usual, just like during the fight against Raios, but by the time all the darkness was absorbed, it was normal again.

Eugeo merely stood and stared at the aftermath of the tremendous battle.

The perfect, spotless marble floor and walls were now melted, burned, and pockmarked all over. In the middle, where the spears of light and darkness clashed, there were fissures in the floor so deep, it was a wonder you couldn't see through to the cathedral level beneath.

No one who wasn't present would have believed that this stunning destruction of the Great Hall of Ghostly Light on the fiftieth floor of Central Cathedral was between just two people, one of whom had been a mere academy student just two days before.

But we did it, Eugeo told himself. *We fought five Integrity Knights of the Axiom Church, the absolute power that has ruled the world since its creation...and won.*

That meant that, including Eldrie, they had defeated nine Integrity Knights so far. According to Cardinal, there were twelve or thirteen knights stationed inside the cathedral. So if they overcame a few more...

Just as Eugeo was savoring the feeling of their progress, Kirito fell heavily to his knees. The black sword tumbled from his hand.

Eugeo hastily let go of the Blue Rose Sword, still stuck in the floor, and helped support his partner's body before it fell over.

"Kirito!"

He was stunned at how light his friend felt, a sure sign of how much blood and life he'd lost. His skin was paler than the marble, and his eyelids weren't popping back open. Eugeo quickly looked him over and then put a hand to the deepest-looking wound, a gash in Kirito's side.

"System Call! Generate Luminous Element!"

He moved the three light elements this produced into the wound and continued the sacred art to unlock their healing power. When the cauterized wound began to seal up, he let go and repeated the process on Kirito's left shoulder. Normally, light elements required a significant amount of spatial resources, and thus a catalyst like holy flower essence, but not in this case. The life the Blue Rose Sword had absorbed from the five knights was now present in the air around them as sacred power.

He had patched up the primary wounds, which would stop the continual loss of life, but Eugeo was not able to use light-based healing arts that could actually recover the amount Kirito had already lost—which was most of it. He clutched Kirito's right hand with his left and began to chant a new art.

"System Call! Transfer Human Unit Durability, Self to Left!!"

This time, motes of blue light appeared all over Eugeo's body and gradually converged on his left hand, through which they traveled to the other youth. Compared to the simplicity of casting the spell that moved life from one person to another, the actual effect was enormous.

Between the fight with Deusolbert and now this one, it was Kirito who had taken all the damage, with hardly anything befalling Eugeo. He could never make up that debt unless he gave back to the point of passing out.

But after half his life had transferred over, or so it felt, Kirito opened his eyes, grabbed Eugeo's hand, and pushed it away.

"...Thank you, Eugeo. I'm fine now."

"No, you're not. You took so much damage, I'm sure there's still more you just can't see."

"It's not as bad as when the goblins got us. I'm more worried about her now..."

His black eyes searched until they saw Fanatio's body lying at the far end of the hall.

Eugeo bit his lip. "...Kirito...she was trying to kill you..."

Just then, he recalled what Kirito had said before he activated his Perfect Control. Eugeo continued, "'You can't win with hatred,' you said. Maybe you were right. That Integrity Knight wasn't fighting out of personal spite or hatred. But...but I still can't forgive what the Church and Integrity Knights have done. If they have both incredible power and the will to protect the innocent people who live here...then why can't they use that power for...for more..."

He stumbled, unable to continue. Kirito got to his feet unsteadily and picked up his black sword from the floor, then indicated that he followed Eugeo's logic.

"They're probably grappling with their own decisions, too. I bet we'll learn more about this if we meet this knights' commander... Your Perfect Weapon Control was incredible, Eugeo. *You* were the one who beat the knights. You have no reason to hate Fanatio as a person or the Four Whirling Blades anymore..."

"As a human…Yeah…I suppose you're right. I was able to understand that much while we were fighting. She was as strong as she was *because* she was human," Eugeo mumbled. Kirito chuckled and agreed.

"They would insist that they stand for absolute good, and you'd think they were absolute evil, but both sides in this equation are flesh-and-blood humans. Absolute good and evil can't be determined by regular people."

Eugeo got the feeling that Kirito was saying this as much to convince himself as anything else.

Kirito, think about how furious you were about that Administrator…Can you still hold the same opinion when it comes to the absolute ruler of the Axiom Church and the entire world?

But before he could actually ask the question, Kirito took off walking for Fanatio, who was still collapsed before the far doors. After five or six steps, he turned back and rustled in his pockets for a little bottle.

"Whoops, nearly forgot. Use this to cure the kids' poison. Just make sure you break their knives and remove any other suspicious tools they might have before you give it to them."

Eugeo caught the bottle, realizing that he'd forgotten about them, too. He pulled his sword from the floor and turned back to Fizel and Linel, who were both still sprawled out and paralyzed. The frost was totally gone from the area now, and the girls didn't seem to have taken any damage from the ice vines or beams.

When he made eye contact with them, they averted their eyes (the only part of their bodies they could move) in a sulking fashion.

Lamenting that he wasn't likely to get along with them, although for very different reasons than with Fanatio, Eugeo knelt down and pulled the two poison swords out of the ground where Kirito had stuck them. Then he tossed them up, so that they spun end over end in the air, and smashed them both with one swing of the Blue Rose Sword.

They shattered easily and melted into little particles of light before they even hit the floor. He sheathed his sword, knelt again, and began patting the girls down for more weapons, apologizing as he did so.

Lastly, he pulled the stopper out of the vial and split the remaining three-quarters of the bottle between Fizel and Linel. Like Eugeo, they would recover from the poison within ten minutes.

He could have simply left them there, but he tried to imagine what Kirito would tell them, and decided he would give it a shot.

"...Knowing you two, you might be tempted to think that Fanatio and Kirito are as strong as they are because they have Divine Objects and Perfect Weapon Control at their disposal... but you'd be wrong. They're strong to begin with. Their hearts are strong, not their techniques or weapons, and that's how they can fight through such terrible pain and perform such incredible feats. You girls might be skilled at killing people. But killing and winning are completely separate things. I didn't understand that, either, until today..."

The girls were still refusing to meet his gaze. Eugeo didn't know if he was getting through to them at all. He wasn't good at dealing with children, anyway.

But even then, the two girls *must* have felt something, watching that fight. It was hard to think of Fizel and Linel as representing absolute evil, given the innocent, childlike way they reacted to things. Eugeo gave them a brief good-bye, then turned and trotted after Kirito.

As he made his way through the devastated hall, Eugeo glanced left and right, checking on the condition of Fanatio's four knights. All four were still collapsed, significantly injured by the indiscriminate light-beam attack. But in keeping with their lofty title, none of the Integrity Knights had lost their full life. They had bled little, and they would probably be moving again before too long.

But unlike her companions, who merely suffered from the beams' minor explosions, Fanatio had taken the full brunt of that charging spear of darkness. Her critical condition was clear from a distance, judging by the large puddles of blood surrounding her prone form.

Eugeo came to a stop near Kirito, who was kneeling at her side. He held his breath and looked over his partner's shoulder at the knight.

Up close, Fanatio's wounds were so hideous that he could barely stand to look at them. There were four puncture wounds on her torso and legs from the beams, her right arm was shredded from the thorns, and she was burned by the aftereffect of her own final attack. Every bit of her was in tatters.

But the most devastated part of her was, of course, her upper stomach where the Gigas Cedar's blow landed. There was a deep gouge the size of a fist pumping blood out constantly. Her face, eyes closed, was so pale that it had almost taken on the color of her armor. She didn't even look alive.

Kirito had his hands over Fanatio's stomach in an attempt to repair her wound with sacred arts. That her Stacia Window wasn't open was probably a sign that he didn't think it was worth looking at the actual amount of life left. He sensed Eugeo's approach without looking up and said, "Help me, she won't stop bleeding."

"Uh...sure," Eugeo said, and he knelt on her other side and put his hands to the wound, too. Like he had done to Kirito earlier, he chanted light-based healing sacred arts. It seemed like the flow of blood was weaker after it, but still far from stopping.

It was clear that if they kept doing this, they would eventually use up all the resources in the area and be unable to generate more light elements. They could temporarily refill some of Fanatio's life by giving her theirs, but it would be meaningless if they didn't stop the bleeding. They needed either a more powerful arts-user or some legendary healing herb to save her now.

Eugeo watched Kirito purse his lips in worry, then eventually decided it was time to say it.

"It's no good, Kirito. She's losing too much blood."

Kirito hung his head for a little while, then rasped, "I know... but if we keep trying to think of an idea...we're sure to find a way. C'mon, Eugeo, help me."

Eugeo was struck by his powerlessness, and it particularly

reminded him of how he had felt two days ago when he'd been unable to prevent the evil acts that befell Ronie and Tiese.

But no matter how hard he thought about it, there simply wasn't any way to call back the life that was vanishing before their eyes. For a moment, he even considered healing the four other knights instead for extra help, but they clearly didn't have the time for that. If either Kirito or Eugeo stopped healing her, Fanatio's life would run out within a matter of seconds. And even if they continued, the only difference was that the moment would arrive in a few minutes instead.

Eugeo summoned his determination and told his partner, "Kirito, when we escaped from the underground cells, you said that we needed to be prepared to kill any enemy who came across our path if we wanted to keep going. That's the mindset you had going into this battle, right? You knew that one side would live and the other would die when you used that attack? At the very least, I don't think Fanatio had any hesitation. It looked like she was risking her entire life. And I think you know, too, Kirito... that this isn't the point where we can go easy on the enemy out of concern for them and actually win."

Ultimately, that was what it meant to use a real sword on someone else, not a wooden one. It was a lesson Eugeo had learned through personal experience; cutting off Humbert's arm had left his hands trembling, his eye in agony, and the pit of his stomach frozen with fear.

He'd always assumed that his black-haired partner had understood these things for ages, ever since they met in the forest of Rulid.

Kirito clenched his teeth and shook his head. "I know...I *know.* She and I fought our hardest...It was a true duel, one where either of us could have won. But...she'll be gone if she dies! She lived for over a century...worrying, loving, agonizing...and I can't just erase that soul of hers. I mean...if *I* die, I just..."

"Huh...?"

"If *I* die, I just"...*what?* Everyone was beckoned up to Stacia's side and disappeared when their life ran out. Kirito might be mysterious in many ways, but he was still human and subject to that universal rule.

But Eugeo's moment of confusion was cut short when Kirito abruptly looked up and shouted, "Can you hear me, Commander?! Your vice officer is going to die! Or prime senator, whatever that is! If any of you can hear me, come down and help her!!"

His voice echoed faintly off the distant ceiling and died out meekly. But he kept shouting.

"Anyone…I know more of you Integrity Knights are up there! Come and save your companion! Priests, monks…*somebody* come!!"

Up above, the disfigured representation of the three gods simply stared down at them in silence. No one was coming—not even the slightest breeze stirred the air.

Back on the floor, the color continued draining from Fanatio's hair and skin. Her life was down to a hundred, or maybe fifty. Eugeo considered suggesting that they observe a moment of silence for Vice Commander Fanatio Synthesis Two as her soul departed for the heavens, but Kirito wouldn't stop screaming.

"Please…someone! If you're watching, help us! Oh…Cardinal! Come quick, Cardi…"

He abruptly fell silent, as though the words caught in his throat. Eugeo looked over at him, and he was surprised to see in his face a transformation from astonishment to hesitation, and then to determination.

"H-hey…what is it?"

But Kirito didn't answer. He stuck his hand through the collar of his black shirt—and pulled out a small bronze dagger hanging from a thin chain.

"Kirito!" Eugeo shouted on impulse. "You know that's—!"

Eugeo had one around his neck, too. Of course he wouldn't forget the daggers Cardinal had given them before they left the Great Library. The daggers had no attack capability, but the target of the blade would be temporarily connected to Cardinal. They were their ultimate weapons. Eugeo would use his on Alice—and Kirito, on Administrator.

"You can't do that, Kirito! Cardinal said there were no extras after these! It's for the battle against Administrator..."

"I know that..." Kirito groaned. "But I can save her with this. I can't have the one thing that will help her right here and simply choose *not* to use it...I can't just assign a priority order to people's lives like that."

He stared down at the dagger in his hand, equal parts pained and determined. Then he quickly but carefully stuck it into Fanatio's left hand, which was relatively unscathed.

Instantly, the blade and the chain shone bright.

Before there was time to draw a breath, the dagger dissolved into numerous little strings of purple light. On closer look, the strings were actually lines of the sacred runes that appeared on Stacia Windows. The fine little lines of text broke free and swooped through the air, then vanished into spots all over Fanatio.

The dagger vanished completely, and purple light enveloped the Integrity Knight's body. Eyes bulging at this astonishing phenomenon, Eugeo belatedly noticed that the blood oozing from the wound in her upper torso was totally dry now.

"Kirito..."

Eugeo was going to point this out, but a voice from nowhere cut him off.

"Good grief. I should have known with you."

Kirito's face shot upward. "Cardinal...is that you?!"

"Time is short. Don't ask the obvious."

That combination of sweet voice and irritated tone could only belong to the previous pontifex they'd met in the Great Library.

"Cardinal...I'm sorry...I—," Kirito stammered.

"Don't apologize to me now," she snapped, cutting him off. *"Given what I've seen of how you fight, I had an inkling that this might happen. I understand the situation—I will heal Fanatio Synthesis Two. But I will have to bring her here, as full recovery will take some time."*

The purple light covering Fanatio's body flashed brighter. Eugeo had to shut his eyes, and by the time it was safe to look again, the Integrity Knight was completely gone—and to his surprise, so was the pool of blood on the floor.

There were a few of the little strings of sacred text still floating in the air. They blinked in synchronization with the sound of Cardinal's voice, which was getting quieter.

"I'll be brief, as the insects are starting to catch on. Based on the situation, there is a high likelihood that Administrator is not in a waking state at the moment. If you can reach the top floor before she wakes, you can eliminate her without needing the dagger. Hurry...there are few Integrity Knights remaining..."

Eugeo could sense that the invisible corridor to the Great Library was rapidly closing. Cardinal's voice grew distant, and just before it faded out for good, the light in the air flickered, then fell to the ground.

Instead, what landed on the marble floor was two little glass vials. Kirito gazed emptily at the azure liquid for a while before reaching out to pick them up. He looked at Eugeo and dropped one in his partner's open palm.

"...Sorry for getting out of hand, Eugeo."

"No...you don't need to apologize. Though I was kind of startled." Eugeo chuckled, eliciting a grin from Kirito at last. He got steadily to his feet and flicked the stopper out of the vial.

"We'd better accept these generous gifts while we can," he said.

Eugeo followed his partner's lead, opened the vial, and downed its contents. It was not at all tasty, kind of like a bitterly sour siral water without any sugar in it, but it was like a douse of cold refreshment to a mind exhausted by so much battle. The substance was healing their damaged life rapidly, the wounds on Kirito's limbs shrinking moment to moment.

"This is amazing...She could have given us more than just the two, though," Eugeo commented, which earned him a shrug from Kirito.

"It would take too long to send such a high-priority object as dat...er, through sacred arts. I'm actually impressed she pulled that off in such a short— *Whoa!*"

Eugeo swiveled to look at Kirito in surprise. "Wh-what?"

"Eugeo...um...don't move. I mean, don't look down."

"Huh?"

Of course, saying so just made it harder *not* to look down. Eugeo's head automatically craned toward his feet. He spotted something that had appeared there without drawing their attention until now.

"Yeep!" he shrieked.

It was about fifty cens long. A long, flat body divided into narrow ringed segments was flanked by a multitude of little legs, about half of which were resting on Eugeo's shoe. At the tip of what was likely the head was a line of at least ten little red eyes, and on either side, a frighteningly long set of needlelike horns, each one waving on its own. It was probably some kind of insect, but it looked more bizarre than disgusting. There were plenty of bugs around Rulid, but none looked like this.

With Eugeo frozen in surprise, the mystery creature waved its feelers around for about three seconds, then began climbing from his shoe up his pants in earnest. He shrieked again and jumped.

"Yeep...!!"

He stomped his foot. The bug fell, landing on its back, then flipped over and promptly scuttled between his legs. Eugeo leaped up and down several times, trying to keep himself away from the creature—and eventually, tragedy struck.

With a crisp *crack* and the sensation of something snapping and squishing underfoot, Eugeo's right foot came straight down on the thing.

Bright-orange liquid spurted in all directions, releasing a sharp, pungent odor. Eugeo nearly fainted when he saw the severed legs still attempting to crawl, but he used superhuman effort to avoid passing out or vomiting. He looked up to Kirito for help.

But his trustworthy partner was now a good three mels away and backing up quickly.

"H-hey...hey! Where are you going?!" he demanded, his voice cracking.

Kirito just shook his head, face pale. "S-sorry. This isn't my kind of thing."

"It's not my kind of thing, either!"

"Bugs like that always come the same way: You kill one, then ten more show up."

"Don't you dare say that!!"

Eugeo lowered his waist, ready to leap onto Kirito and take them both down together, when a purple light suddenly flashed below him, causing him to freeze again.

Beneath his shoe, the wretched remains were evaporating into light. Within a few seconds, the spattered gunk and broken carapace were totally gone. Eugeo felt the soothing calm of deep relief.

Noticing from a distance that the danger had passed, Kirito returned rather matter-of-factly and noted, "...Ah, right, I see. That must be one of the familiars that Administrator has prowling around, looking for Cardinal. I bet it smelled the connection to the library..."

"..."

Eugeo glared up at Kirito with no small measure of hatred, then gave up and replied, "So...you're saying there's a bunch more of those things crawling around the tower? I've never seen anything like it until now."

"Remember how there was that shuffling on the other side of the door when we escaped into the library from the rose garden? They're probably good at hiding—and I'm not gonna try snooping around to find them. Plus, Cardinal said something strange...about Administrator being in a non-waking state or something..."

"You're right, she did...So she's sleeping? In the middle of the day...?" Eugeo wondered.

Kirito rubbed at his chin and answered doubtfully, "Cardinal said that Administrator and the Integrity Knights were making certain sacrifices to be able to live for centuries. Administrator in particular sleeps almost the entire time...but it makes me wonder how she's controlling the bugs and the knights..."

He looked down at the floor for a while and then scratched at his bangs as he murmured, "But I guess we'll find out the answer when we go up there. Anyway, Eugeo, can you take a look at my back?"

"H-huh?"

Kirito spun around before he could react. Baffled, Eugeo's eyes slid across the black fabric, which looked tattered from the rigors of so much battle but was otherwise normal.

"Um...I don't see anything wrong..."

"I'm just wondering...Do you see a little bug on it? Kind of a spidery thing."

"No, nothing."

"Okay. That's good. Well, let's start the second half!"

Kirito started walking for the huge doors at the north end of the hall, and Eugeo had to rush after him.

"Hey, what was that all about?!"

"Oh, it's nothing."

"Well, now I can't help but be worried! Look at my back now!"

"Trust me, you shouldn't be concerned."

They proceeded onward, bickering and joking like they'd done ever since Rulid, but deep down, Eugeo practiced the question he really wanted to ask.

If you're always so calm and collected all the time, what made you so distraught about Fanatio's death? What was supposed to come after, "If I die, I just..."?

Kirito...who are you...?

The swordsman in black stopped at the massive doors several times his height, reached out with both hands, and heaved them open. A gust of cold air rushed to meet them, and Eugeo had to turn his face away.

3

Beyond the double doors was a chamber about the same size as the entrance hall they came up through on the southern end of the Great Hall. It, too, was rectangular, with long, narrow windows on the far wall that offered a view of deep-blue sky.

But the black-and-white-patterned stone floor was missing one crucial element: the staircase that would take them to the fifty-first floor and above. They looked all over, but there wasn't even a hanging rope, much less a ladder. There was only a strange circular recess in the stone floor, and Eugeo couldn't see a single thing that suggested a way up.

"No...no stairs," he mumbled, following Kirito farther into the dim room. The flow of cold air across the back of his neck made him hunch his shoulders. His partner noticed it, too, and they both looked straight up.

"...Wha...?"

"What is that...?"

Then they fell silent.

There was no ceiling. There was just empty space in the same shape as the room itself—no, a vertical shaft—that stretched up as far as the eye could see. The top was lost to thick darkness, making it impossible to tell how high it went.

As their eyes traveled slowly back down to ground level, they realized that the shaft was not just a smooth, hollow space. Along the side of the shaft, at heights corresponding to the levels above, were doors leading to each successive floor, albeit smaller than the double doors they'd just come through. Extending from each door was a narrow little terrace that stretched about halfway across the shaft.

So all they had to do to infiltrate the floors above was get to those terraces. In a daze, Eugeo reached out and jumped into the air.

"…Of course I can't reach it…," he mumbled. Even the lowest of the terraces was higher than the ceiling of the Great Hall of Ghostly Light, well over twenty mels overhead.

Next to him, neck outstretched, Kirito asked weakly, "Listen… Just checking here, but there aren't any sacred arts for flying, right?"

"Nope," he answered without pity. "Only the Integrity Knights have the right to fly. And they use flying dragons, not sacred arts…"

"Okay…Then how do the people here get up to the fifty-first floor and higher?"

"I don't know…"

They puzzled over that one together. Just when it seemed like they would have no choice but to turn back to the Great Hall and ask Fanatio's subordinates for help, Kirito whispered, "Something's coming."

"Huh?"

Eugeo looked back up the shaft.

Something was indeed approaching. A dark shape was coming slowly down the shaft, nearly grazing the uniform edges of the vertical line of terraces. They jumped backward out of the way, and Eugeo watched the shadow descend closer, hand on his sword hilt.

It was a perfect circle about two mels across. Given the way the edges glinted in the blue light from the narrow windows, it appeared to be forged from steel. But why was this object just float-ing slowly down the shaft without any visible means of support?

As the disc passed the terrace two floors above, speed steady the entire way, Eugeo began to hear an odd hissing sound. Again, he was aware of cold air flowing over the back of his neck.

He could neither run away nor draw his sword, but stood in place dumbfounded as the disc brushed the terrace overhead and descended toward them. When it was just a few mels away, he noticed a small hole in the middle of the disc's underside that was emitting little bursts of air, which explained the strange sounds and breezes.

But how could the power of wind alone keep such a large metal platter floating in the air? The object's hissing grew louder and louder as its descent gradually slowed, until at last it came to fit perfectly in the circular depression in the middle of the floor with a soft *thunk*.

The top of the disc was polished as smooth as a mirror. There was a finely decorated silver handrail placed around the rim. In the center of the disc was a straight glass tube about one mel tall and fifty cens wide. Next to the tube was a girl, with both hands resting on the bulged spherical end.

"...?!"

Eugeo took another step backward and squeezed the hilt of his sword. He tensed, ready for the revelation of a new knight.

But very soon, he realized that the girl was not equipped with so much as a knife anywhere on her body, much less a sword. And she was wearing a long black skirt that seemed unsuited to combat. The white apron from chest to knees with an under-stated crochet pattern around the edges was about the most decorative element in her outfit, and she had no articles or acces-sories otherwise.

Her grayish brown hair was cut straight across at eyebrow and shoulder level, and the features of her pale face were unremarkable. They looked fine but lacked character or expression. She appeared a bit younger than Eugeo, but there was no way to be sure.

Eugeo gazed at her eyes, wondering who she was, but they were downcast, the lashes covering them so that he couldn't even make out their color. She folded her hands in front of the apron, still not looking at either of them, and bowed deeply before saying at last, "Pardon me for the wait. What floor will you be visiting?"

It was a voice devoid of emotion and with only a bare minimum of inflection. At the very least, there was no hostility, either, so Eugeo took his hand off his sword. He repeated her question.

"What...floor? Are you saying that you're going to take us higher up?" he asked, scarcely believing it.

She lowered her face again. "That is correct. Please tell me the floor you wish to visit."

"Um...well..."

Eugeo wasn't sure what to say; he'd grown to assume that anyone they met in the cathedral would be an enemy. Next to speak was Kirito, who was often just as inscrutable in his own way.

"Well, um, we're wanted men who snuck into the cathedral... so are we allowed to ride on this elev—I mean, this flying disc?"

The girl's head tilted the tiniest bit in confusion, then returned to position. "My job is merely to operate this floating platform. I am under no other orders."

"I see. In that case, we'd be happy for a ride," Kirito said, walking right up to the circle.

Eugeo called out, "H-hey! Are you sure about that?"

"Well, it doesn't look like there's any other way to get up."

"Uh...I guess you're right, but..."

After what the two child knights did to them, Eugeo was stunned that his partner could be so trusting again, but on the other hand, they had no clue how to operate the disc. He simply had to tell himself that if it was a trap, they could somehow jump to the nearest terrace.

They stepped onto the disc through a gap in the delicate handrail. Kirito peered at the glass curiously and told the girl, "Well, uh, take us to the highest floor this can go."

"Yes, sir. Ascending to the Cloudtop Garden on the eightieth floor. Please keep your hands and feet behind the guardrail at all times," she replied, bowing, and put her hands on the top of the tube.

Then she sucked in a breath and said, "System Call. Generate Aerial Element."

Eugeo's first instinct was that she was about to attack them with sacred arts, but he immediately realized he was wrong. The shining green wind elements appeared inside the clear tube. But it was the number that amazed him—a full ten, which marked her as a considerable master of the arts.

The girl lifted her right thumb, index, and middle fingers off the glass tube and murmured, "Burst Element."

Three of the elements flashed green, and a rumble started under their feet. With all three of them on top, the metal disc began to rise as though lifted by an invisible hand.

"Aha! So that's how it works," Kirito exclaimed, and thus the pieces clicked into place for Eugeo as well. The tube running through the middle of the disc released wind elements, pushing the explosion of wind downward and propelling the disc and the weight of its three passengers upward.

It was very simple once they knew how it worked, but the movement of the disc was so smooth that they barely felt it. Aside from a brief feeling of pressure at the start, it essentially floated up without the slightest bit of movement.

The marble floor dropped farther and farther away, and it hit Eugeo that this floating disc was going to take them to the eightieth floor of the cathedral—in other words, an elevation up in the clouds. He wiped his sweaty palms on his pants and clenched the handrail.

Kirito, meanwhile, was taking it all in stride as though he'd ridden on such a thing before. He made sounds of admiration as he examined the disc, and when that was done, he turned his attention to the person operating it.

"How long have you been doing this job?"

With just the faintest note of surprise in her voice, the downcast girl replied, "This is the one-hundred-and-seventh year since I received this Calling."

"A hund—?" Eugeo gaped, forgetting about the distance under their feet. He took over for Kirito and asked, "Y-you've been moving this floating platform for…a hundred and seven years?!"

"Not…all that time. I receive a break for lunch, and I do rest at night."

"Er…that wasn't what I meant…"

But perhaps it did explain what he wanted to know. Like the Integrity Knights, her life had been frozen so that she lived atop this little plate of metal for what was essentially eternity.

The disc rose, slowly but surely. Whatever emotions the girl might have had, she kept them hidden. As one wind element ran out, she released another, then another, each time with the command, "Burst." Eugeo wondered how many times she had said that word before and realized that he couldn't imagine it.

"Hey…what's your name?" Kirito asked suddenly.

She put on her most pronounced display of confusion yet. "My name is…forgotten. I am simply called the operator of this platform. My name is…the Operator."

Kirito was unable to mount a reply to this. Eugeo counted the terraces as they passed, and by the time he reached twenty, he felt an impulse to say *something* to break the silence.

"…Um…so, listen…We're going up there to defeat a very powerful person in the Axiom Church. The person who gave you this Calling."

"Is that so?" was her only reply.

But Eugeo pressed on, knowing that his words probably meant nothing. "If…if the Church disappears, and you're released from this Calling, what will you do…?"

"…Released…?" she repeated awkwardly. The girl named Operator was silent for a whole five terraces.

Eugeo glanced up and saw, to his surprise, that the gray ceiling was now in sight and approaching. That would be the base of the eightieth floor. At last, they were reaching the central core of the Axiom Church.

"I…I do not know anything but the world of this shaft," the girl blurted out. "Therefore…I cannot possibly choose what my next Calling should be…but if I had a wish…"

For the first time, she lifted her face and stared through the narrow windows on the right wall, out to the pure-blue sky.

"…I wish that I could fly this platform out there…wherever I could go…"

Eugeo saw, now that they were visible at last, that her eyes were the absolute crystal blue of midsummer sky.

Just before the final wind element flickered and died, the disc reached the thirtieth terrace and slowly floated to a halt. The Operator removed her hands from the glass tube, folded them in front of her apron, and bowed.

"Thank you for waiting. This is the eightieth floor, the Cloud-top Garden."

"…Thank you."

Eugeo and Kirito bowed back and stepped onto the terrace. She dipped her head briefly one more time, looking down again, and as the wind element weakened, the platform began to descend. That rustling sound of the wind expelling faded, and eventually the tiny, confined world of metal trapped in time was gone.

Eugeo lamented, "…And I thought my old Calling felt endless…" Kirito shot him a look, eyebrow raised, so he explained, "At least I was lucky enough that I could retire after getting too old to swing an ax. Compared to what she's been doing…"

"Cardinal said that even if you freeze the natural degradation of life, you can't prevent the soul from aging. Eventually your memories start to crumble, and then it all falls apart in the end," Kirito said, downcast.

He turned around, forcefully cutting off that line of thought, and faced away from the long vertical shaft. "What the Axiom Church is doing is wrong. It's why we've come all this way to put

a stop to Administrator. But that's not the end of it, Eugeo. The real problem is what comes after..."

"Huh...? Weren't we going to leave things up to Cardinal after we beat Administrator?" Eugeo asked. Kirito's lips moved as he sought the right thing to say, but there was a rare moment of hesitation in his eyes. He turned away.

"Kirito...?"

"...Actually, I'll tell you the rest after we get Alice back. This isn't the time to be thinking about extra stuff."

"Well...okay, I guess," Eugeo replied. Kirito hurried down the terrace to escape his gaze. Eugeo followed after him, feeling no small amount of apprehension about what had just been mentioned, but the sudden surge of tension that gripped him when he saw the large doors ahead swept away his concern.

Given how many Integrity Knights had been waiting for them on the fiftieth floor, it seemed clear that whoever was giving the orders—Fanatio had mentioned a prime senator—intended to put a stop to them right then and there. It was practically a miracle that they had withstood the furious assault of the knights and won.

Now that they had broken through that barricade to threaten the top floor, this prime senator would use whatever power necessary to stop them. They might open this door and come across the commander of the Integrity Knights with all the remaining members, flanked by powerful priests and monks to cast sacred arts from a distance.

But there were no side routes in. Whatever awaited, they had to meet it head-on.

Kirito and I can do this.

They shared a look of determination, reached out to the doors, and gave a push together. The large slabs rolled inward.

"...!"

The resulting combination of color, trickling water, and sweet scent was so overwhelming that Eugeo couldn't believe his senses at first.

They were still inside the tower. The same white marble wall as the rest of the obelisk was visible in the distance ahead. But the floor here was no longer stone tile; instead, it had thick, soft grass. Here and there bloomed holy flowers, which were the source of the scent.

To Eugeo's surprise, there was even a pristine little brook a short distance away, its surface sparkling. From the doorway ran a narrow brick-lined path that crossed over the brook with a wooden footbridge before continuing on.

Beyond the river was a small hill. The path snaked its way up and over the slope, which was covered in flowers. Eugeo followed the trail with his eyes all the way to a single tree standing at the top of the hill.

It wasn't a very big tree. The thin branches supported dark-green leaves and little orange cross-shaped flowers. The light of Solus coming through the windows just below the high ceiling fell right on that tree, illuminating the flowers like gold.

The slender trunk also shone in the sunlight—and at its base was a flash of even brighter gold…

"Ah…!"

Eugeo didn't even register the gasp that came from his mouth.

From the moment he saw the girl resting against the trunk with her eyes closed, he failed to think of anything else.

Like some trick of the gentle, dappled sunlight, the girl's entire form shone with gold. The beautiful armor that covered her top half and arms was already dazzling gold to begin with, and her long white skirt had embroidered highlights of similarly colored thread. Even her polished white leather boots seemed to radiate in the sunlight.

But more beautiful and glowing than anything else was her long, flowing hair. It was perfectly straight, running from her perfectly curved head down her back, like a waterfall of holy light and molten gold.

Years ago, he had seen that hair every single day. He had tugged on it and jammed twigs into it, innocent and ignorant of its glory and fragility.

That golden shine that was a symbol for friendship, longing, and just a tinge of love, turned in the course of a single day into a reminder of Eugeo's weakness, ugliness, and cowardice. Now the light that should have remained forever out of his grasp was in reach once more.

"A...Ali...ce...," he mumbled, scarcely hearing the words. He lurched toward her, wobbling down the brick path. Eugeo couldn't even sense the pleasant fragrance of the holy flowers or the babbling of the brook. The only sensations that connected him to the rest of the world were the warmth of his sweaty hand clutching the collar of his shirt and the pulsing sensation of the little dagger beneath the fabric.

He crossed the bridge over the water and started up the hillside. Less than twenty mels to reach the top.

As he looked up, he saw the downward-facing features of the girl, clear as day. There was no expression of any kind on that pure white skin. She just sat there, eyes closed, floating in the warmth of the sun and the scent of the flowers.

Is she sleeping?

If he snuck up on her and held out the dagger to prick one of the fingers resting on top of her knees...would that be the end of it, right there?

Just then, Alice raised her hand, and Eugeo stopped, his heart leaping into his throat. Her shining lips opened to let him hear that familiar voice.

"Please wait just a little longer. The weather is so nice, I want to let her soak in the sun a bit more."

Her eyes, bordered by golden lashes, slowly opened.

Irises a shade of blue that existed nowhere else in the world met Eugeo's gaze. He anticipated a softening in her look, the hint of a smile to play over those lips.

But the blue of those crystal eyes was not gentle like it once was. It was the color of permanent ice, unmelting under centuries of sun. Eugeo was trapped in place, an intruder caught in the sights of a sentinel.

So battle would be unavoidable.

Lost memory or not, she was Alice Zuberg from the village of Rulid, and now he would have to point his sword at her—to return her to normal. No matter how hard and unforgiving the fight would be.

He understood the strength of Alice Synthesis Thirty, Integrity Knight. He'd learned it by experience, when she smacked him in the face with her scabbard. He hadn't merely been taken by surprise; he hadn't even seen the blow before it landed. How difficult would it be to neutralize a warrior of such skill without hurting her, either?

She could not be fought with anything less than his greatest effort.

But can I even manage to cut a single lock of her golden hair?

He couldn't take a single step forward, much less draw his sword for battle.

While Eugeo struggled like never before, Kirito approached from the rear and murmured hoarsely, "You shouldn't fight, Eugeo. Just think of how to stick Alice with Cardinal's dagger, that's all. I'll block her attacks with my body if I have to."

"B-but..."

"It's the only way. The longer the battle goes, the worse our odds get. I'll take Alice's first hit on purpose, hold her down, and then you use the dagger. Got that?"

"..."

He bit his lip. In the fight against Deusolbert, and again versus Fanatio, it had been Kirito who suffered all the bloodletting. And this mad rebellion against the Axiom Church had all stemmed from Eugeo's own personal desire in the first place.

"...Sorry," he muttered, feeling abashed.

"You don't have to apologize," said Kirito, sounding more normal now. "I'll give it back to you double...But, that aside..."

"...? What is it?"

"Well...based on what I can see from here, she doesn't seem to be armed. Plus...who was she talking about...?"

Eugeo focused on Alice again, sitting atop the hill. She had closed her eyes and put her head down again, but sure enough, that golden whip from their encounter at Swordcraft Academy was nowhere to be seen.

"Maybe she's on break and left her sword somewhere else… Boy, wouldn't that be helpful," Eugeo hoped, without any audible conviction.

Kirito brushed the hilt of his black sword. "I feel bad, but we can't wait for her to stop napping in the sun. If we attack now, whether she has her sword or not, she won't have time to cast her Perfect Weapon Control. If there's one thing we need above all else, it's to prevent that from happening."

"Good point…My Perfect Control doesn't use up too much of the sword's life, so I think I can use it two more times today…"

"That'd be great. But one more's the limit for me. And we should have this knight's commander after Alice, too. Anyway… here goes."

Kirito signaled to him, then took a step forward. Eugeo summoned his courage and followed.

They stepped off the brick path, which wound around the hill, and headed straight for the top. Their boots rustled the grass. When they were halfway up the slope, Alice stood. Through half-open lids, her emotionless, icy gaze met them.

Instantly, as though her vision itself could cast sacred arts, Eugeo felt his legs turn to lead. Despite the lack of any weapon, Eugeo's legs seemed to be refusing to get any closer to Alice. Was that one bash to the cheek enough for his body to have learned its own subconscious lesson? Yet it seemed like Kirito's pace was losing steam up ahead, too.

"…So you have come all this way up at last," Alice's crystal-clear voice rang out. "I made the decision that even if you should somehow escape your cells, Eldrie would be enough to stop you cold in the rose garden. Yet you defeated him, and then Deusolbert with his divine weapon, and even Fanatio, before setting foot in the Cloudtop Garden."

Her arched brows darkened. There was a faint note of mourning from her cherry lips. "What in the world is giving you your power? Why do you seek to unravel the tranquility of our realm? Why do you not understand that for every Integrity Knight you harm, a major weapon against the forces of darkness is lost?"

It's for you. That's all this is, Eugeo thought. But he knew that this statement would mean nothing to the Alice facing him now. He clenched his teeth and put all his concentration into moving forward.

"I suppose I shall only have my answers by the blade. Very well...if that is what you seek," she relented, placing her hand on the trunk of the tree.

But she has *no blade*, Eugeo protested, right as Kirito mumbled, "No way—"

There was a flash of light, and the little tree sitting atop the hill vanished.

"——?!"

A moment later, there was a rush of thick, sweet fragrance, and then it was totally gone.

In Alice's right hand was now a familiar longsword. A weapon made entirely of shining gold, from blade to hilt to sheath. A cross-shaped pattern of flowers decorated the hilt.

Right in that moment, Eugeo didn't understand what had happened.

The tree vanished, and the sword appeared. Did the tree change *into* the sword? But Alice did not give any commands. Whether it was a simple illusion or some kind of ultra-high-level matter-conversion art, it should have been impossible without a verbal command.

But...not unless the tree changed its form based on only Alice's thoughts, making it...

Kirito reached the conclusion a split second before Eugeo did. He snapped, "Dammit, that's not good...Her sword might *already* be in Perfect Control mode!"

Alice stared down at the stunned boys, holding her sword flat with both hands. She drew it crisply, the blade a deeper golden yellow than the sheath, gleaming as it reflected the light of Solus.

In an instant, Kirito was rushing forward. Whatever power it was that Alice's sword held, he was determined to force close combat before she could utilize her Perfect Control over it. He tore up the hill, blades of grass flying, and crossed nearly the entire distance within ten steps.

Eugeo tried his hardest to follow after his partner, still clutching the chain around his neck. Kirito wasn't going to draw his weapon. Like he said, he was going to block Alice's first attack with his body, which would give them just a tiny amount of time to hold her back. It was absolutely imperative that Eugeo take advantage of that window to hit her with the dagger.

Nothing in Alice's expression changed with the black swordsman charging up at her. She calmly, almost carelessly, pulled her sword back.

Kirito wasn't yet within sword range. Was it a ranged attack, like Deusolbert's and Fanatio's? If so, she might stop Kirito at a distance, but it would still leave Eugeo with enough time to get in close with the dagger.

Eugeo peeled off from Kirito and kept running at a different angle.

Alice's right hand swung forward—and the golden blade disappeared.

"?!"

It did not actually disappear. It was more like a disintegration. The sword split into hundreds, thousands of pieces that hurtled at Kirito like a golden storm.

"Aaagh!!"

Kirito was knocked clean off his feet by the shining swarm. Eugeo gritted his teeth and raced onward, determined to make use of the momentary diversion his partner created.

But the golden wind did not stop there. With a sound like rustling leaves, it abruptly darted left in midair to engulf Eugeo next.

The force was irresistible. It felt like a giant swatting him with the palm of its hand, knocking him over on his right side.

Each individual fragment, less than a cen in length, was tremendously heavy. Eugeo instinctually covered his face with his left arm as he landed on the grass and felt a searing pain there. It was all he could do not to scream and roll around in agony.

The swarm of gold pieces, having easily stopped them, flew back to Alice's side, where they hovered around the knight rather than returning to sword form.

In fact, on closer examination, all of the shards were cross-shaped combinations of even smaller diamond-shaped pieces. It was the same as the design on the hilt of the sword—the shape of the flowers from the tree.

"Are you mocking me? Why else would you run for me without drawing your weapons?" she asked, still without the slightest hint of emotion. "I held back on that attack, as a warning. The next time, I will eliminate your life. Use all the power you possess, for the honor of those knights you already defeated."

She…held back? And that tremendous power was the result…?

As Eugeo watched in horror, the golden flowers audibly bristled with metallic sounds in unison. The tips of the petals, which had previously been rounded and smooth, were now sharper than the end of a rapier. It wouldn't just be a body blow anymore; those points would split the skin and sever bone.

Deep fear plunged Eugeo's limbs into numbing, icy water. Even a single one of those golden flowers could take his life down to dangerous levels if it struck the right spot—and there were at least two or three hundred circling around in the swarm. It was impossible to deflect them all with a sword, and probably just as difficult to evade the practically sentient multitude. Alice's Perfect Weapon Control was almost *too* perfect, and all-powerful…

Yes. It was too perfect.

Perfect Weapon Control of a Divine Object was very powerful, but even that had its limits. The core of the power was extracting the "memory" of the weapon's material and turning it into an exaggerated physical property: heat, cold, toughness, speed. For it to specialize in one area, by necessity it had to sacrifice power in others.

Fanatio's Perfect Control was so developed in terms of compressing light to that powerful beam that it was overturned by Kirito's simple mirror response.

Whatever the nature of the little tree that was the core of Alice's weapon, if the sum of its potential was split among so many tiny objects—focusing on accuracy—then the attack power of each individual petal must be small. It just didn't add up that those little objects less than a cen across could have the weight of a giant's fist.

In order for that to be possible, the slender little tree with orange flowers had to be an ultra-high-priority object, even more powerful than the Gigas Cedar that was the basis for Kirito's sword…

Nearby, Kirito lifted his head, his face a pale mixture of astonishment and horror as he arrived at the same conclusion as Eugeo. But not knowing the meaning of the word *resignation*, he turned determined eyes toward Eugeo and mouthed, *Chant*.

Getting through the storm of petals by orthodox methods was impossible. The only way was to immobilize the actual wielder through the Blue Rose Sword's own Perfect Control. Earlier, Alice was swinging around the naked hilt to match the movement of the flowers. That suggested that the mass of petals wasn't moving solely of her own control.

From his prone position, Eugeo subtly laid a hand on the hilt of the Blue Rose Sword and began to recite the Perfect Control chant at a barely audible level. If Alice noticed him and attacked, he'd be totally defenseless, but Kirito would handle that.

As he expected, Kirito bolted to his feet just at that moment and called out in a loud, deliberate challenge, "I apologize for treating a proud Integrity Knight in a manner lacking in proper respect! Kirito, student of the sword, seeks a proper duel of blade against blade with the Integrity Knight Alice!"

He thumped his right fist against his chest and dipped his head, then grabbed the hilt of his sword from his left side. After drawing his pitch-black weapon with a vicious *shing*, he held it up in a stance, as if to split the golden aura that surrounded the knight.

Alice gazed at him, her blue eyes all-knowing, then blinked and said, "Very well. I shall ascertain the nature of your wickedness from the way you fight."

She motioned with the hilt. With a sound like waves, the cloud of golden flowers gathered within reach like a little dust devil and assembled themselves into the shape of a perfect, unbroken blade. They made a *ch-ching!* sound and fused, returning to the form of that golden sword.

As she approached, regally holding her sword at chest level, Kirito moved his blade low and said, "It is inevitable that one of us will fall once we cross blades. Before that happens, answer me this: I see that your divine weapon takes its form from the tree that was on the hilltop previously. How does such a small tree hold such incredible power?"

It was obviously a stall for time, but Kirito really did want to know the truth behind the golden sword's Perfect Control. Eugeo was curious, himself. He listened in as he continued reciting.

Alice took three steps forward before coming to a halt. She paused, then opened her mouth to speak.

"It would be pointless to tell you just before you die…but I suppose I shall do you this favor on your path to Heaven. The name of my weapon is the Osmanthus Blade. As the name suggests, it was once nothing but a simple osmanthus tree."

Osmanthus was a type of small tree that bloomed tiny orange flowers in the fall. It hardly grew at all around Rulid, but Eugeo had seen a few in Centoria. It certainly wasn't a one-of-a-kind specimen like the Gigas Cedar.

"As you said, it is merely a small tree—except for its age. The place where Central Cathedral stands now was once, in the distant past, the Place of Beginning, which the creation goddess Stacia gifted to humanity. In the center of the little village was a beautiful spring, with a single osmanthus tree growing on its bank...according to the first chapter of Genesis. That tree is the origin from which this sword was forged. Do you understand? This Osmanthus Blade is the oldest thing in existence."

"Wh-what...?" Kirito gasped.

She continued, "This sword is a reincarnation of the tree that God herself placed. Its quality is 'everlasting eternity.' Even a single fallen petal will split stone and tear the earth where it lands... just as you experienced for yourselves. Do you now understand what it is you face?"

"...Yeah, I get it," Kirito replied obligingly. "So it's the first indestructible object that God placed, huh...They just keep upping the ante with these things they pull out. But I can't waste my time being amazed by it."

He brandished his black sword high, now seemingly rather insignificant in comparison to a tree-based weapon of a much higher notoriety. "Integrity Knight Alice...let us fight!"

The black swordsman leaped off the ground, audibly ripping his way through the air. He charged with such speed that it was hard to believe he was the one going uphill.

Kirito likely believed that if he could start his combination attack within close range, no matter what Alice's weapon was, he could seize the advantage. Fanatio's ability to respond in kind was a product of her unique personal mastery of the combination arts and surely was exceptional among the knights.

As Kirito and Eugeo expected, Alice pulled her sword back overhead in honest response to Kirito's high slice. She couldn't block him if he segued that high attack to a mid-level one next.

The downward burst of black lightning met with the Osmanthus Blade, sending up pale sparks.

But the second attack did not instantly emerge.

Alice's sword barely budged, but Kirito bounced backward, as though he had tried to smash a boulder with a stick, and lost his balance.

"Whoa..."

The slope played havoc with his feet, forcing him to take several wobbly steps, while Alice pursued with the grace of rushing water.

Her left hand extended fully, all the way to her fingertips. The golden sword drew back straight behind her, leaving her front wide open. It was an old-fashioned style, not nearly as practical as the Aincrad style, but between the flowing blond hair and waving skirt, there was a kind of painterly beauty to the sight.

"*Eiii!*" she cried, swinging the sword forward in a semicircle. The speed was tremendous—but the movement was too grand.

Kirito had recovered his balance and had plenty of time to hold up his sword.

Grakk! The two swords clashed. Once again, it was Kirito who spun away from the impact like a top. He put a hand to the grass to avoid falling off his feet as he slid down, nearly to the foot of the hill.

At last, Eugeo understood the nature of what he was seeing. The weight of each blow was off the charts.

With his high-priority divine weapon and special Aincrad combination attacks, Kirito had bested a number of Integrity Knights to this point, but the Osmanthus Blade was likely several times heavier than Kirito's black one. At that speed, it was hard enough just to survive the attack, much less deflect the impact.

And that wasn't all. As the first impact had proven, even when Kirito was the one attacking, he wound up getting knocked off balance. The outcome was obvious.

Realizing this for himself, Kirito scrambled to his feet and took several hasty steps in retreat. Alice glided after him.

It was as one-sided a fight for Kirito as had ever happened in the last two years.

With her flowing, methodical beauty, Alice attacked again and again. The young man did his best to block and was knocked around miserably each time. He might have fought back had he been able to dodge, but for the great size of her swings, Alice's aim was extremely fast and accurate, such that Kirito could never evade her cleanly.

Eugeo finished his command, following the two with bated breath. He would have to unleash his Perfect Weapon Control while his friend was still able to block the attacks.

After just five blows, Kirito was already pressed up against the western garden wall. There was nothing but hard marble behind him and nowhere else to run.

Alice pointed the tip of her sword at her trapped foe, expression as cool as ever, and said, "I see. You are only the second to evade my strikes for so long. No doubt, you have great determination and belief that propelled you up the tower. But you are far short of destabilizing the Church. And I cannot allow you to endanger the peace of the realm."

There was no weakness to exploit in the golden knight's regal stance. Even from behind, Eugeo felt that she could react and stop his sacred arts.

Say something, Kirito. I just need a moment, a chance, Eugeo thought as he ran, but his partner just glared at her fiercely with his back to the wall and held his silence.

"Then prepare yourself," she said, lifting the Osmanthus Blade up to point straight at the heavens.

There was a moment's silence.

Then, with a terrible air-ripping noise, golden light appeared.

Forcing his eyes as far open as possible, Kirito moved his hand at blurring speed.

A metallic clash. Sparks.

He didn't absorb the blow, but he diverted it. Sword met sword at the slightest possible angle, just enough to shift the trajectory of Alice's unfathomably heavy swing.

The Osmanthus Blade ran through a spot just a single cen to the left of Kirito's head: smooth marble wall. A few strands of black hair flew into the air and vanished.

Then he leaped at her. He held down her right hand with his left and locked his other arm around hers. At long last, that succeeded in getting a facial reaction from the previously unshakable Alice.

Now.

"Enhance Armament!!" Eugeo screamed, thrusting the Blue Rose Sword into the grass at his feet.

In an instant, the ground was white with ice. The wave of frost raced forward and swallowed Kirito and Alice where they stood, about ten mels away.

A rush of icy vines grew up their legs. They formed blue crystal chains that wound around the two bodies. Kirito's black clothes and Alice's white armor were soon covered in thick ice.

Kirito, Alice, I'm sorry!

He continued pumping out more and more ice vines. After seeing what Alice could do, no amount felt like enough to hold her down.

The crackling vines gripped tighter and tighter until they eventually changed into a single thick pillar of ice. The giant crystal, multifaceted like a raw gemstone, glistened quietly with the two combatants trapped inside. The only thing extending from the block was Alice's hand and the Osmanthus Blade in it, stuck into the wall. Frozen in time within the blue ice was a look of slight surprise on Alice's face and sheer determination on Kirito's.

One prick of the dagger on her extended arm, and it was all over.

Eugeo let go of the Blue Rose Sword and stood up. The Perfect Weapon Control would be undone now, but that huge block of ice wouldn't melt naturally for many minutes. He squeezed his little dagger and took a step forward, then another...

When his third step landed, golden light exploded.

"Ah...!"

To his shock, Alice's trapped sword was disintegrating into countless petals again.

With a stately, harmonic thrum, the storm of golden flowers circled the pillar. The tiny cross-shaped blades swarmed and chiseled the ice as Eugeo watched helplessly. If he jumped into that fray now, he would lose his life before getting a single step closer.

The flowers shredded the ice until there was just a thin layer left, then fluttered up higher into the air. With a delicate crack, what was left of the ice pillar crumbled to the ground.

Alice thrust Kirito toward Eugeo with the hand that was grappling with him, brushed loose a bit of ice still stuck in her hair, and, as if nothing had just happened, said, "Did you not seek to reach a conclusion through a sword competition? It was an amusing diversion…but mere ice cannot hope to contain my flowers. I will fight you next, so stay there and wait your turn."

She extended her right hand, and the cloud of petals instantly coalesced back into their original—

"Enhance Armament!!" screamed Kirito.

However it was that he had found the time to recite the chant, Kirito's black sword sprayed out darkness.

It plunged not for Alice herself—but for the Osmanthus Blade, just before it was whole again.

"Wha…?!"

For the first time, Alice was startled.

The surge of darkness scattered her golden petals and ruptured her control over them.

With an ear-shattering roar, dueling storms of black and gold rumbled and soared. They tangled, swirled, and slammed against the marble wall behind her.

"*Eugeoooo!!*" Kirito screamed.

That was right: This was the final chance.

Eugeo pulled the dagger from its hiding spot and charged.

Just eight mels to reach Alice.

Seven.

Six.

And then something happened that no one could have predicted.

The abnormal surge of the melded powers of divine Perfect Weapon Control slammed into the Central Cathedral wall so hard, cracks and splits began to form.

With an earthshaking rumble, the massive marble edifice, seemingly indestructible just like the Everlasting Walls, began to crumble.

Squares of stone fell outward one after another, and the hole in the wall grew and grew. Eugeo stared, dumbfounded, at the blue sky and white clouds beyond.

A sudden gust of wind smacked his back and knocked him to the grass. The air inside the tower was being sucked out through the hole in the wall—and the two closest to the aperture were helpless to resist it.

To his utter shock, the tangled black swordsman and golden knight were sucked out of the tower. The image burned itself into his retinas.

"Aaaaaah!!" he screamed, crawling up to the hole.

What should I do? Make a rope from sacred arts—no, use the Blue Rose Sword's ice to—

He didn't have time to put any of these ideas into action.

The stones of the cathedral wall that had fallen through the outside were gathering together, as though time itself were rewinding.

With each one fitting into place, the hole got steadily smaller: *gonk, gonk, gonk.*

"Aaaaaah!!" he wailed again, rushing up to the wall just as it became seamless once more.

He slammed a fist against it. And again. And again.

The skin of his hand split and blood flew from the wound, but the restored wall did not budge.

"Kiriiito!! Aliiiiice!!"

His voice only echoed off the cold, smooth marble.

(To be continued)

AFTERWORD

Thank you for reading *Sword Art Online 12: Alicization Rising*. Beginning, Running, Turning—the Alicization arc is on its fourth volume now, and it's about the time that the conclusion should be coming into sight, but...boy, Kirito and Eugeo sure have been climbing for a while. I mean, Central Cathedral is a hundred-story structure, just like Aincrad, so I guess it must be hard to get up that far. They should be reaching the top in the next volume, so just hang on for a bit more stairs, please!

The *Rising* subtitle for this book, of course, refers to their ascent up the tower, but in English, you don't actually "rise" up stairs, you "go up" them. The next time you students have a sacred arts—er, English test—remember the difference!

It was in April 2009 when the first volume hit the shelves, so with the original release of this twelfth book in April 2013, the *SAO* series has lasted four years. Within the story, the launch of *SAO* is November 2022, and Alicization takes place in June of 2026, so that's about three years and seven months. (And an extra two years for poor Kirito in the Underworld...)

During that time, Kirito, Asuna, and the others have been through a variety of experiences in the virtual world and the real world, and grown as people. As for me, the author, I can't actually think of anything that has changed for me. My personality and living situation are so fixed in place, I have to wonder if Administrator is behind it all! I haven't even changed the laptop

I use to write! (Although the keys are fading from all the typing, I guess.)

I suppose this just means that I fear change and get annoyed by it. I'm more resistant to the idea of changing my surroundings than I am eager to upgrade my PC, and I prefer my weekly bike rides to remain the same, down to the last turn...But if I don't come into contact with new things, I feel like the scope of my stories will narrow down and down, so I'm hoping that this year will be one of change. First thing is to get a new laptop...but gosh, putting the screen protector on is so annoying...

So given these and my other failings, I owe a great debt of gratitude to my editors Mr. Miki and Mr. Tsuchiya; to my illustrator abec, whose work is always executed with aplomb despite his busy schedule; and of course, to all of you readers as we embark on Year Five!

Reki Kawahara—February 2013